Anointed In

Presents

Joyful Noise: The Hot Mess Choir

She Nell

Note: This is a work of fiction. Names, characters, places and incidents either are products of the author's imagination or are used fictitiously. Any resemblance to actual events or locales or persons, living or dead, is entirely coincidental

Anointed Inspirations Publishing is currently accepting Urban Christian Fiction, Inspirational Romance, and Young Adult fiction submissions. For consideration, please send manuscripts to

anointedinspirationspublishing@gmail.com

Dedicated to:

You

Be joyful in hope, patient in affliction, faithful in prayer.

Romans 12:12

Chapter 1

Deidra

It was five minutes before the alarm sounded off. I woke up in a pool of sweat. My satin pajamas clung to my body. My nightmare was all too real. In fact, it was more a reliving of the Wednesday night meeting than a nightmare.

Last Wednesday night we gathered in the choir room to discuss the Mass Choir. There were questions about who would participate in the choir.

"Any member of a choir at Holy Missionary."

There was the question about singers. "What if they are not a lead singer?"

"Doesn't matter."

Then there was the what about the children question.

"They are welcomed."

My favorite was the "With all due respect, First Lady, we don't sing those old tired hymns like the Senior Choir, will we be able to sing some upbeat songs?"

That came from one of the young choir members. That one comment ignited a firestorm and they became the Hot Mess Choir. It took an hour just to get them to settle down.

"Those old hymns are what gets you through," Mother Odell said.

"You right about it, that is what is wrong with the young church. They want to be so worldly, they have forgotten where they came from." Another older member said.

"Forgot, how could we? You never let us forget. That is too fast of a song for church, you say. That song is too loud, you say. Last, I checked the bible said to make a joyful noise." One of the younger members shouted.

"What do you know about what the bible says?"

Those few words started the biggest fight in the choir room.

I maneuvered myself from under the arm of my bear of a husband. He slept soundly. Saturdays are his days to sleep in because he spent so much time during the week pastoring Holy Missionary Baptist Church.

Sitting up in the bed I take notice of his soft almond complexion. He is a beautiful man, even if I cannot stand him right now. It is his fault that I am up this early on a Saturday. Normally, I would sleep in with him and do some light errands in the afternoon. The next nine Saturdays will not be filled with light shopping and lunch with friends.

For the next two months, I am tasked with getting the Holy Mass Choir performance ready. The Holy Mass

Choir is made up of members from each of our five choirs at Holy Missionary. My husband and pastor thought it would be a great idea if we had one choir for the pastor anniversary celebration. Because of my music background, he also thought that I would be a perfect choice for directing this choir.

Because I am working on my Proverbs 31 mentality, I told him I would love to direct his anniversary choir. I even said it without rolling my eyes although I did mumble "this is going to be a hot mess" under my breath. That Sunday afternoon the Hot Mess choir was born.

That Wednesday they fussed about everything from practice times to who would make up the choir.

You would think that a room full of Christian people would be a little more loving. To think, my sleeping husband wonders why I dread getting up and directing his Hot Mess choir.

I slowly slid out of the bed and head to the bathroom to prepare for combat with the Holy Mass Choir. Today will be our first practice. Considering how spirited our first meeting was, I decided to put on some slacks and a cotton polo style shirt. I set my day two twist out free from my satin cap and fluff the flatten curls. Because of great genetics, I barely need to apply makeup and only put on a light coat of foundation, lip stain, and mascara.

Walking back into the bedroom my big bear of a husband watches me finish getting ready.

"Good morning, First lady Deidra Jones." He says playfully with a smile.

"Good morning, Pastor Jones," I reply without a smile.

"Eww, what has you in such a funky mood this beautiful morning sister?"

Although I want to say your Hot Mess choir and this pastor anniversary project you put me in charge of I do not. I took a deep breath and stared into his brown eyes.

"Nothing, just getting ready to leave, you know it is Saturday? I have choir practice before lunch with Sheila."

"Oh okay, well I plan to be home all day getting ready for Sunday's word. I have a couple of finishing touches to add to the sermon. Instead of having lunch with her why not have it with the choir? My treat." He said reaching for his wallet.

As a pastor he did not make loads of money, however, as a property owner, he did very well. So well in fact that I did not have to work my corporate job. I left that world shortly after we were married and enjoy full-time ministry work. I work from home on small projects and tackle big projects like this choir when the need arises.

"What is the topic this Sunday?"

"Faithfulness, how you have to be faithful to God even when it is uncomfortable or something that you don't want to do. We must understand that God has a bigger plan. A plan that is often bigger than us. For example, if you oversaw a mass choir. It would be wrong to call them your Hot Mess Choir because God has a purpose for them."

I blushed and turned away. I know that he is right, but I do not care at this point. He was not at the meeting. I thought I was going to have to break up a fight in the choir room of all places. I was not dressed to fight that day. However, today should it be any trouble, I am ready. I slip on my black Converse and prepare my mind.

Chapter 2

Shonda

I do not know who decided that Mass Choir practice was going to be on a Saturday, but they certainly did not have six children to deal with. No one can understand the amount of laundry I have to do on a Saturday. I would make the boys do it, but the last time that happened I had pink sheets instead of white. I did not mind the pink but Blake my oldest at 16 was not thrilled. That is what I get for letting the twins Bill and Bud do the laundry that week. You would think at the age of 14 they would be able to handle such an easy task. I could have let my baby boy Bradley do it, and things would have been great. He is very smart for an eight-year-old much smarter than his two older brothers Byron age 10 and Bryan who just turned 12.

How in the name of Jesus am I going to get all these boys and myself to the church by 10 am for choir practice? I swear whoever came up with this was not thinking of their members.

"We are ready" the twins sang "the twinors are in the house." They continue to sing their words in chorus.

"Twinors?" I question looking at them puzzled.

"Yes twinors, twin tenors." Bud, who's the oldest by one-minute, answered.

Even though Bud is two inches taller than his twin Bill, they look identical. That is why I make them wear different colors. Today it is orange and brown. Bill has on an orange top and brown bottoms and Bud has on a brown top and orange bottoms.

"I swear you two are some fruits," Blake says as he walks past them in his night clothes and plops in front of the television.

"Mom." The twins yell in unison.

"Blake, leave your brothers alone and get dressed," I yell as I walk into my room to get myself together.

"No, I am not going."

"What?" I stopped in the hall and walked back to the living room. "Yes, you are."

"No, I am not. I am 16, a man, what do I look like on a Saturday going to choir practice? I don't even like going to choir practice when you force me to sing with the babies. What I look like going today?"

"You look like a child that lives in my house. As for me and my house, we will serve the Lord. Now get up off my couch and get dressed." I said as he got up and walked past me. "And by the way, the only man in this house is Jesus and He went to the temple." I walked back to my room to finish getting myself ready.

Although I have six kids you would not know it by looking at my body. With each of the boys, I was able to snapback as my grandmother would say. I look a lot like her thin and short about five feet five inches. She had 13 kids one of them being my mother. I inherited her long hair and her flawless complexion. My brown skin is so smooth that I never wear makeup. With six boys to run after there is not much time for it anyway.

A master in the kitchen, Bryan had breakfast made before everyone was up and complaining. That was one less thing for me to worry about. I guess the laundry would have to wait until we got back home although I planned to put at least one load in before we left.

Byron and Bradley are the last of my tribe to wake up this morning. They are both easy going boys and do not give me much trouble. Both take after their dads. Dwayne, Bryon's dad was a good guy and I really messed things up when he caught me cheating with Bradley's dad. Dwayne was a nice guy he took care of me and my then four boys. He did more for them then their daddies. Bryan's dad has been missing ever since I told him I was having his child. The twin's dad got locked up shortly after they were born and is still doing time in prison. Blake's father is just a jerk and I try to have as little to do with him as possible. Lucky for me I got saved and Jesus and I have been raising these boys for the past 10 years. So, I am unsure who little Mr. Blake thinks he is, but he will be in the house of his father this morning at 10 am.

Looking at my watch I see that I have less than 30 minutes to get my tribe to church. Lord, I need an extra dose of strength. I did not sleep last night waiting for Blake to come home. He was out at a football game with his friends. He could have played this year, but his grades were not where they needed to be to make him eligible. I tried to encourage him but that fell on deaf ears. I guess no one wants to hear from their mom when things like that happen. I was heartbroken when he told me because he is so talented, but I understood.

I have had several fights with him about his grades and his future. Again, nothing has worked to change his passion for school. If I would let him, he would probably be on the street corner hanging out all night with his friends. I do not like his friends. When I asked him to invite them to church, Blake laughed at me. That was the sign for me that they were not the type of friends he needed.

As I walked from my room to the bathroom to tame this wild hair I pass the twins in the hall singing. They sound amazing together as they sing unto the Lord. Blake yells at them to be quiet and Byron copies him. Byron looks up to his older brother and wants to be just like him. I wouldn't have a problem with that if Blake made better choices. After I tame the frizz that is my hair, I apply a little makeup for the first time in a while. I tried not to look as tired as I felt.

"Ma, I thought you said we had to go. What are you doing?" Blake questions as I continue to fix my face.

"Boy, what does it look like I am getting ready."

"Ma, you don't need to get fancy, there is not anyone at that lame church that wants you."

"What. Boy, you better remember who you are talking to. I don't do it for attention like them fast girls you run after. I do it for me." I said staring at his reflection in the mirror.

With that said I finished my hair and loaded my tribe into the van. It is 9:50, I have ten minutes to get to a place 20 minute away.

"Jesus be a fence." is all I can say as I drive out of the garage.

Chapter 3

Donnell

I can hear my neighbor banging on the wall of his apartment. He wanted me to turn down my music that is blasting. Reluctantly, I go to my Bluetooth speaker and turn down my Jesus music. If I was bumping some mainstream, I hate women, let's get high, where is my gun at music I could understand but this is gospel. This is Gospel Hip Hop. Which in my opinion is much better than that other stuff. I am not sure who thought it would be a great idea to have practice at 10 am, but I don't need to be at work until 4 pm so I am okay with it.

Normally, I would work out but since I needed to be at practice I guess that was off the list this Saturday. I will have to take a day during the week to hit the gym if I want to stay my fit self. Mondays are out of the question because that is when the young adult choir practices. I have been a member of the Young Adult Choir since college. I was so blessed to find a church like the one I attended back home when I came here for college.

Holy Missionary has been a great place to worship and I am glad I decided to stay after finishing school. Currently, I am a manager for a small firm which requires me to work one weekend a month. If I did not have to work today I would call up some of my boys and hang out.

After I turned down my music I go to the kitchen to make breakfast. Mama raised her only boy to do it all, so I make myself a mini gourmet breakfast. Once that is done I head to the closet to see what I will wear. Because I have a great job my closet is what some women would die to have. I actually have two huge walk-in closets in my spacious bedroom. One closet is where I store my workout equipment it is like a mini gym. The other is for my clothes and is the smallest of the two, although it is still very big.

Getting dressed is easy when your clothes are color coded and separated by style. I chose a pair of jeans and a polo. I matched my shoes to my shirt and gave myself a once-over in the large mirror. My daily workouts have paid off. I noticed my muscles even while clothed.

"Looking good man of God, looking good."

I had plenty of time to chill before I needed to leave so I decided to call and check on my daughter. She lives with her mama. Tiffany, my baby's mother, and I met in college. She did not finish after she had Eva.

Eva is three and is the light of my world. I wish I could spend more time with her and have her come live with me, but I know that Tiffany would not have it.

Tiffany represents that one fall from grace. We all have them, and she is mine. I was in my sophomore year and chilling with some of my fraternity brothers after a party. We were all hanging outside of the party watching the people leave. I knew I should not have been there, I had church in the morning. But that was a time when I had one foot in the house of the Lord and one in the streets.

Tiffany and a group of barely dressed girls walked by us. The area was so packed that she was stopped right in front of me. I could smell her perfume and it smelled like heaven.

"You not going to say hello?" I asked.

"Hello, and you are?"

"Donnell."

"Well hello, Donnell."

"You are?"

"Tiffany."

When she said her name, it was like the sweetest thing I had ever heard. She was about 5 feet 8 in her heels. She wore a blue dress that showed off her curves. Her long weave went down to her round butt and I was caught in her spell. She gave me her number and told me to call her that night.

Although I was in a getting to know you relationship with Sister Stacy at church, I called Tiffany anyway. That was my first mistake. My second mistake was going to her house that night.

Within moments of my arrival, we were both naked in her bed. After that night I did not hear from Tiffany for three months. When she called it was to tell me that she was having my baby.

This broke Stacy's heart and she never spoke to me again. Even though we go to the same church and sing in the same choir, she still will not speak. I have tried everything I know and nothing. Losing Stacy is my regret but having Eva is my saving grace.

I love my little girl and hope that one day I can make a family with Stacy and Eva.

"Hello."

"Hey, I was calling to check on Eva."

"She is fine."

"Look I was wondering if I could pick her up and take her to church with me?" I asked Tiffany.

"No, you not about to have your church hoes up in my baby's face. Besides me and her new daddy got plans."

"You listen here, as long as I live I will be the only daddy she has I don't care how many men you let sleep in your bed."

Tiffany must have heard the anger in my voice because she hung up the phone. That is fine with me because God as my witness I am going to get my baby Eva and Stacy back.

Chapter 4

Mother Willie-Mae Odell

"Lord, these children have lost their minds. I am way too old to be getting up, and out the door before 10 am. I bet any amount of money that First Lady is going to be late. I am sure the young people will fall into the church after 10 am. Lord, have mercy on these old bones." I am unsure why I always speak to this empty house.

Grabbing my teeth from the nightstand, I shuffle to the bathroom. I may be old, but I am far from helpless. I slowly take my rollers out of my hair. I need my grey curls to last until Sunday. I decide not to comb or brush them down. Miss Thang aka First Lady should have known better than to have practice on Saturday.

If she would have paid attention to the list of traditions and protocol that I gave her this would not have been an issue. For years our choirs have practiced during the week. The Senior Choir has practice on Tuesday. The Young Adult Choir has practice Monday. The Adult and Children Choirs have practice on Wednesday. The men have practice Thursday. Nobody has church on Saturday! That is the way we do things at Holy Missionary Baptist Church, where Reverend Myron Jones is the pastor, unfortunately.

I am not sure where the board got these two from but to God be the glory. I consider wearing my floral dress or my striped dress. Shuffling to my drawer, I select some pantyhose. "I better get a move on," I say to my husband's picture as I close the drawer.

He, Albert, has only been gone three years and I miss him every day. My fast tail daughter thinks I should date but I told her the Lord has a greater calling for me. I don't have time to chase or run from men at this juncture in life. I told her, "I got to do the Lord's work." Right now, that work means protecting the church from these outsiders trying to change stuff.

All my years at the church we ain't never had no Pastor anniversary day. Reverend Long was there for 45 years and not one time did we say happy anything. Now they want to say happy anniversary, for what! That boy has only been a Pastor for a year!

I pull my pantyhose over my chunky legs, I have put on some weight since Albert passed. About 50 extra pounds, making me 250. Being only 5'4 the doctor is concerned. I told him just like I told my daughter not to worry, the Lord is in control. More people should rest in the Lord instead of trying to do so much.

These church folks being the main ones. Looking at the clock I notice that I have about an hour before I must leave my retirement community and head to the church. I shuffle to the kitchen to make something to eat.

I am not that hungry, so grits, eggs, sausage and butter toast is all I cook. I must admit it is hard being here alone with only the Lord at times. Although, I would not rather be with anyone else.

I decide as I eat to go over the song selection for this Hot Mess Choir. "Yea, I said it," I say to Albert's other picture on the wall. This is not going to be a Holy Mass Choir. This is going to be a Hot Mess Choir. Whenever you mix up God's plan it is bound to be a hot mess. God had instructions for our founding members. Each choir sang on a certain day. Each choir practices on a certain day. That is the order that God set up for Holy Missionary Baptist Church.

Now, this Jones fellow has children singing with adults and young people singing with old. We do not want to sing any of those songs the young choir sings. Truth be told, I hate going on Young Adult Choir Sunday. If you ask me, they need to have an altar call all service that Sunday.

I shuffle back to the kitchen to wash my dishes. I make sure my floral dress looks okay in the reflection from the mirror in the hallway. Looking at the clock I have just enough time to make it to the church on time. I decide to ready my spirit with some worship music in the car as I drive to church

"Lord please do not let your children work my nerves, this day. In Jesus mighty name I pray. Amen"

As I pull in to the church with my worship music playing, I notice the First Lady getting out of her car. Well, at least she is on time I began to smile to myself until I got a glimpse of her outfit. My mouth flew open in disbelief. Certainly, the wife of Reverend Myron Jones, Pastor of Holy Missionary Baptist Church knows better. I sit in my car and watched her sashay into the church. Miss thing has done it now, and I just got out of prayer with the Lord. How dare she walk in the house of the Lord in her position as First Lady in pants!?

Chapter 5

Deidra

I got to the church on time, thank God. As I walked through the doors of the church I could feel someone staring at me. I looked around but did not see anyone. I am still very self-conscious. It has not been easy for my husband and me. Holy Missionary Baptist Church has some deep traditions. My husband, God bless his heart, seems to think he can make a difference. I am unsure if that is possible. The traditions at Holy Missionary Baptist Church run deep.

While standing in the choir room I hear a person clear their throat as they stand behind me. I must admit I am a little frightened as I turn around slowly to find Sister Odell standing behind me with folded arms.

"Sister Odell, I did not know you were here. Hello, how are you." I said with a smile.

You would have thought I cursed in church if you judged my hello by her facial expression.

"Excuse me, my name is MOTHER Willie Mae Odell. You can call me Mother Odell but never sister!" she said with her hands on her hips.

"Pardon me, Mother Odell," I said like a scolded school girl "I meant no disrespect."

She rolled her eyes and walked to her seat as other members started to enter the room.

I decided that it was best if we did a roll call of choirs to ensure that every choir was represented. Not wanting to leave the musicians out, I started with the drummer. As soon as I called his name he began to play a funky beat. As I called each instrument they joined in playing. I began to jam to the music. When I called the Young Adult Choir they began to jam with me. The Adult Choir was a little offbeat, but it did not matter we were having fun. Then I saw the crossed arms and scowls on the faces of the Senior Choir. If looks could kill Mother Odell would have shot me. As her eyes bore through me, I stopped swaying to the music and adjusted my clothes.

I called the Senior Choir and they said present in one loud disapproving voice. As I called for the Children's Choir the door flew open. A disheveled Shonda and her six boys rushed into the choir room.

"Here is the children's choir now," Donnell whispered smirking. "Ouch," he said as Sister Stacey elbowed him in his rib for making fun of Shonda.

Shonda did bring in half of the choir but that was mean for him to mention in his condescending tone. It was clear to see from the way she rushed in that she had a tough time getting the boys to church. I was just grateful that she made it to the ten o'clock practice. I was surprised that all of the choirs made it and most where on time. I thought with all the bickering they were not going to come out.

As we begin to go over song selections the keyboardist asked if we would consider an original song that he wrote.

"Hel-Heck naw we are not doing no worldly song you thought up!" Mother Odell shouted before I could answer. The young man looked as if someone had stolen his favorite possession.

"We would love to hear your song sweetie," I said as I shot my own death ray with my eyes at Mother Odell. "Can you prepare it for our next practice and we will vote. That brings me to the song selection. We will practice six songs and decide which three we like the most. We have three selections during the celebration." I said taking command of the room. I could tell by the astonished look on Mother Odell's face that she was not happy. I'm not sure how this Proverbs 31 thing is supposed to work but she is getting on my nerves already.

The first song we sang was messy. Voices were all over the place. The seniors sang really high and the young adults sang really fast. The poor adult choir was totally offbeat and the children, all I can say is bless their hearts. I stopped them and ask that we take a five-minute break. "Let us give the little ones a potty break." Unsure of what I was going to do with this hot mess I went to the corner of the room.

As I stood contemplating my role as a First Lady a quiet and meek Sister Stacey walked over to me. Dressed in her modest skirt and blouse she asked if she could have a word. I said yes, of course, she was one of the few people in the church that liked me.

"First Lady D," she began in her sweet voice, "maybe instead of sitting with our choirs we should sit in our sections. You know altos with the altos, tenors with the tenors etc."

She was like a ram in a bush. That was an amazing idea even if Mother Odell would not agree. Which of course she did not agree. She mumbled under her breath as she moved from one side of the small room to the next. She rolled her eyes at me as we began to sing the same song for the third time.

After two hours my energy level was down. Dealing with squirmy kids and mean adults made me tired. I ended the practice and informed everyone that we would meet next Saturday at the same time. That, of course, led to groans from some of the members, but I was too tired to care.

I sat in my car as the members drove away thinking about what I have got myself into. With tears filling up my eyes I reached for a tissue in my purse and saw my husband's credit card. Just then I remembered that we were supposed to have lunch. The only person left in the parking lot was Mother Odell and I certainly was not going to ask her.

Chapter 6

Shonda

Going to choir practice and then to the grocery store with six boys is no laughing matter. Between the pranks and play fighting I am tight-roping on my last nerve by the time we pull into the driveway. To their credit, the boys are good about helping unload the car. Each of them grabs a bag or two as they head into the house. Although they are great about unloading the car, they are not great when it comes to putting the groceries away. As they walk by the kitchen they pile bags on the counter and continue to walk in their rooms.

I am so frustrated by this point I don't even argue. I throw on some gospel hip hop and get to work. My music drowns out the sound of video games and play fighting. Once the items are all put away I head to my room to get some rest.

"Mom can I borrow the van," Blake says as he walks into my room. He looks so innocent and sweet like he did when he was a baby.

"To go where?" I ask not fooled by his appearance.

"Well me and the guys wanted to hang out and we have the biggest car, so I figured I would drive." He said sheepishly.

"Who is the guys? Ronnie and them?" I asked as he nodded, still trying to look like a boy scout. Blake is not a bad boy and Ronnie and them are good kids but they are still kids.

"Mom please, you can trust me, and I won't be gone that long." He begs.

I am not sure if it is the fact that I am tired or his pretty brown eyes, but something makes me tell my sixteen-year-old it's okay.

"Back by midnight!" I yell as he heads out of the door.

After I feed the remaining children and get them in their beds I settle down to read. First, I read a couple of scriptures from my Bible, which is worn and tattered. After reading the first couple of chapters of Romans I decided I would crack open a new novel. I have been meaning to read "A Good Thing" and think now is a good time.

Mid-way through chapter 3 I notice that the house is very quiet. I look over at the clock and it reads midnight. Certainly, I think to myself Blake will be pulling up in the driveway any minute. I peacefully returned to the pages of my book.

Turning the pages of my book I noticed that I am now on chapter 5 and Blake has not walked in my house. I try to call his cell phone, but it goes to voicemail. My heart begins to race. I have a young black male child out in the street past midnight. We, unfortunately, live in a society where that could mean a hundred dangerous things. I try his cell phone again and still it sends me to voicemail. Thoughts of police brutality and gang violence fill my mind. Blake knows how to be respectful to the cops and is not in a gang but that does not stop my mind from having wild thoughts.

Just as I pick up my phone to call the police I hear the van pull up in the driveway. I put the phone down and slowly sit on the couch as he walks in the living room. He fumbles with the keys and is giggling to himself. I watch him as he staggers from the door into the living room.

"Oh shoot, ma!" he giggles "I did not see you, how you this evening?" He questions with a half-smile as his brown eyes dance in his head.

"Boy are you drunk, did you drive my car drunk, have you lost your mind?" my questions come at him at once with no break causing his head to swim. He staggers to the couch to sit. I stood over him.

He cannot look at me in the eye. No matter how many times I yell at him to do so, he won't look at me. I continue to yell for another minute or so before I realize that he is too drunk to comprehend anything I am saying. The other boys have heard the yelling and now they are up and standing in the hallway. Furious I yell at them to go to bed.

My skin hurts and is hot I am so mad at my son. He could have killed himself or worse someone else. I am unsure where I went wrong or what he is thinking. I just stared at him as he sat on the couch slumped over looking lost.

Before I cursed him out or stuck him I took a deep breath and headed to my room. I slammed my bedroom door so loud it shakes the house. God, where did I go wrong I wonder? Sure, Blake's dad wasn't around but I kept him and all the boys in church. I don't have liquor in my home, I try to expose them to the things of God and I make sure that they know the Lord. But despite my efforts, Blake is just determined to be the opposite of what I am trying to raise. I am so hurt that I tearfully pray myself to sleep.

In the morning I find a sleeping Blake slumped over on the couch in his same clothes from the night before. I yelled his name to shake him out of his peaceful slumber. Startled he wipes the drool from the side of his face and looked around for my voice.

I can tell that his head hurts by the way he holds his hands over his ears. I yell even louder knowing that it hurts him. I, in fact, yell for the next hour about the pitfalls of underage drinking and driving. I yell until he is in tears and swearing that he will never touch a drink again. I am lucky that my disappointment still holds some value, but I am unsure as to how long that value will hold. As much as I hate to admit it Blake is growing up, they all are, and the world is a tough place for a young black boy.

Chapter 7

Donnell

I watch Stacey walk to her car in disbelief that she still is not speaking to me. Sure, she says hello, but nothing more than the normal everyday greetings. We used to be very close before my mistake and I am determined to repair what I have done. As she drives away I can't help but kick myself again for messing up what we shared.

Since I have a couple of hours before work I decide to spend my energy at the gym. My workout is intense but not enough to get my mind off Stacey. As I run my standard three miles I thought of her soft brown skin. As I lifted weights I thought about her soft natural hair that I use to play in as we watched movies. Nothing I did would take my mind off this girl.

I decided that I would give her a call on my way to work but she did not answer her phone. I hesitated as I left a dry message on her voicemail.

"Hey, this is Donnell I was wondering if we could grab a bite to eat and talk," I say. "Let me know."

This girl has drove me crazy.

After work, I did what any heartbroken man would do I find the one girl that I know loves me. I pull up to

Tiffany's house desperate to see my daughter, Eva. I knock on the door willing to slay her beast of a mother to see my princess.

"What you want?" Tiffany asked as she came to the door dressed in short shorts and a dingy tank top.

"Eva," I said brushing past her and walking into her cluttered home.

"No, you did not just walk yo' dusty behind up in my house. Boy, I am busy."

"Doing what, watching the Housewives on television?" I said looking at the TV.

"No" she lies "I was cleaning."

I can tell from the amount of debris on the ground that she was not cleaning.

"Where is Eva?" I ask just as she runs around the corner in her nightgown.

I know that she must have had it on all day because it is far too early to be ready for bed. The pink gown is dingy as if she has been playing outside in it. I look at her mother and shake my head.

Eva's hair was uncombed, and she had dirt on her pretty caramel skin. I go to the kitchen and wet a napkin despite the sink full of dishes.

"Let daddy clean your face baby," I said to my princess.

"When is the last time you did her hair?" I question her mother who just throws her hands up and walked away.

I move several papers and clothing from the couch. Sitting down I grab my little angel and a comb from the floor. Taking out her matted ponytails I gently comb her hair while we watched television.

"Did you turn the channel from my television show?" her mother asked.

"Yea, she does not need to be watching that stuff and you said you were cleaning," I said looking around the house.

I continued to do Eva's hair while we watch a friendly children's program. I section each part of her head and comb it. I put her cute hair bobbles on each ponytail. Her hair is partly clean. I make a mental note to wash her hair the next time she comes over to my house. After doing her hair I read to her and she falls asleep in my arms.

"Give me my child so I can put her to bed," Tiffany said.

"I got it," I said as I lift Eva up and take her into her room.

I must step over toys and clothing to get to her bed. I feel myself growing angry. I shut Eva's door and head back into the living room. Tiffany can tell by my facial expression that I am not happy.

"Don't start with me Donnell, you don't know what it is like being a single mother." She said as she throws up her hand and walked away.

"Forget that man, what about being a woman period. Look at this place you cannot tell me you are happy living like this. Tiff, you got to do better." I said for Eva's sake.

"Well for my sake you need to go. I got a lot to do before my new man gets here."

"New man?"

"Yes, my NEW man. The last thing I need is you here when he arrives. Trust me you don't want to be around tonight cause some freaky mess is going down. You know how I do. You remember you ain't as holy as you think you are." She says as she presses up against me.

What I ever saw in her I do not know. I peel her off my chest and head to the door stepping over shoes and papers.

"You know you still want me." She said.

"No, I do not," I replied as I walked out of her home.

What I wanted was Eva out of this situation and Stacey back in my life. But God has not given a brother the desires of his heart at this time. As I went to my car I called Stacey again. But she did not answer.

Chapter 8

Mother Odell

In all my church years I ain't never seen nothing like Miss Thang. Miss First Lady D as she has the children calling her. I cannot believe that she was bopping to the music during choir practice. She had everyone hyped in the Lord's house like this was some sort of nightclub. In all my church years I have never seen such a display. It is obvious what needs to be done.

"Hello Edith, this is Mother Odell. Yeah, I know we just saw each other at choir practice. Anyway, that is why I am calling. I am having a Senior Choir meeting at my house today,6 pm. Call everybody on the list. Okay, I will see you at six. Yes E, I will have food."

I rush to the grocery store to pick up some chicken and other items. I saw that poor Sister Shonda struggling with those six boys of hers, but she does not see me. Thank God! I would not want to have to make conversation with her and her rough looking crew. I am sure she does the best she can do but Lord knows she can do better.

By the time I get home, there is enough time to change clothes and put out the feast. I bought fried chicken and macaroni salad at the grocery store. I already had a lemon cake that I sliced up and placed on a tray. If it is one thing I know about the Senior choir is they love to eat.

We were a group of saints ranging from age 55 to 100. That's right we have a member 100 years young that is still going strong. She will be here for sure, so I make sure to put out extra throw pillows. She needed some extra support for her back.

Just as I put the last few touches on my home the doorbell rang. Choir members arrive on time ready to eat and discuss. I allow everyone to get their plates and say hello before I begin to speak.

"If I can have everyone's attention. I called this meeting so that we can talk about this Hot Mess, I mean Holy Mass Choir."

"You said it right Hot Mess." One of the senior choir members said.

"Well, it would appear that we are mandated to do this, however, we can decide how we are going to it. We do not have to agree with no hippy hop foolishness. We do not have to agree with no dancing and shaking during the Lord's worship."

I received a few "Amens" from the members.

"So, what are we going to do about it?" A member asked.

"We are going before the Pastor and the Elders of the church. Miss Thing needs to be brought before the board."

"Mother!" someone shouted, "do you think that is necessary."

"Yes, I do. In fact, I know that it is! It is the only way we are going to take our respect back and shut down this Hot Mess Choir."

Several of the members agreed with me and the ones that did not agree were outnumbered so they did not matter.

"Mother let me remind you that if we are going to do this we must follow protocol. We must call a meeting after practice with Lady D and the Holy Mass Choir first. We have to do this before we can see the Elders." One of the senior members said.

She was right, protocol did dictate that we do things that way.

"Okay fine we will have a general meeting after the next choir practice. Maybe Miss Thing will get the hint and we can end this Hot Mess Choir." I agreed.

With our agreement made, the members began to leave my meeting. Some still talking about the Hot Mess Choir and others talking about the practice we just left.

I was very satisfied that my issues with Miss Thing would soon be over. This is just what she needed to keep herself in check – to be sat down. After our meeting with the choir and then the Elders, I am sure she will be out of my hair. Nobody likes or needs a First Lady that is up front. The First Lady should be silent and in the background.

She is prancing around like she is a role model for the young women. The only model they need to follow is Jesus. Not some pants wearing, arms showing, bopping so-called First Lady. She had some nerve at practice today in pants of all things. Truth be told she was far too happy and had too much sway to the music.

I decided to put on my butter beans from last night before I take off my clothes. I changed into a house dress and turn on the TBN Channel. I thank God for blessing me with free cable and the 700 club. Just as I get ready to eat my beans and rice my phone rings.

"Hello," I said slightly annoyed.

"Hello Mother Odell, this is Lady D. I mean this is Lady Deidra. I hope I am not disturbing you?" she said.

"Well, I was about to eat. What do you want?"

"Well, I just wanted to tell you that I am glad to have the senior choir be a part of the Holy Mass Choir. I know that is out of the box, but I know it is going to be a blessing to the church. I am sure God would be pleased to see us all come together."

"Oh, okay that's nice. Well like I said I was about to eat so I will see you at church." I said and hung up.

How dare she call my phone and tell me what would make my Jesus proud. She obviously does not know who she is dealing with. I am Mother Willie Mae Odell. I am fully aware of what pleases the Lord and it ain't her!

Chapter 9

Deidra

"Why did you make me do that!" I whispered loudly across the table to my husband.

"Because it was the right thing to do." He said.

I stared at him and his light brown eyes stared back at me. I dare not challenge him although my flesh wants to. I take notice of his greying beard and his soft face. He is lucky he is cute, and I love him. Turning away to eat my salad I roll my eyes.

We decided to go to lunch after choir practice. I was slightly offended that none of the choir members wanted to attend lunch. Everyone left in a hurry. My bear came to my rescue and offered to go with me. He said it would give us a moment to talk. I must be honest I was more interested in venting to Shelia, but she and I decided to take a rain check.

I needed to spend this time with my husband. Things at this church have been very different from our old church. We knew that taking this assignment was going to be difficult. Holy Missionary Baptist Church has been in existence for longer than I have been alive. They are rich with traditions. As my aunt would say their roots run deep.

We did not come from a church built on tradition. Our former church was built on the Word of God and that alone. We had choirs and praise teams but they all loved one another and there was no internal fighting amongst the groups.

This cannot be said for Holy Missionary. You would think the choirs were rival gangs at times. They wear their robes like gang colors. Once there was an argument because a new member to the Young Adult Choir picked up a Senior Choir robe by accident. That was like a mini world war in the choir closet. Each member had taken sides and proceeded to yell at the poor girl. Why she did not quit the choir I do not know? That would have been my cue to exit.

I tried to explain my frustrations to my husband who sits across from me listening and nodding. He took a deep breath as if he is taking all of the hot mess in and he puts down his fork. I sat up in my seat to prepare myself for his words and counsel.

"Sounds a bit messy." He said as he continued to eat.

I stared at him as if he had two heads. A bit messy you think, I wanted to say. You have me dealing with these folks and you know it is a bit messy, I want to say.

"Really, that is all you have to say." I finally broke my silence.

"Look, Dee, I know it is a hot mess as you like to say, but God has a purpose for the choir." He said taking my hand.

"But babe, why not just do a choir showcase and let them sing separately?" I begged looking as sweet as I could given my frustration.

"Nope, that is not the vision. We are one body. They will make a joyful noise with one voice or I will sit every choir down."

"That might be better," I mumbled.

"What was that First Lady?" he questioned me with a look of disappointment.

"Nothing it is just that they honestly do not like each other. It is like each choir thinks they are the only choir and that Mother Odell is the ringleader. I can't believe you had me call her."

"I had you call because you win more flies with honey. She just wants to be heard and respected. Mother Odell is alright she is just steeped in tradition and a little misguided. But one thing for sure, she loves the Lord and so do you."

"Loving the Lord aside, Myron she hung up on me. Now I do not know what I did to that woman and I do not care. Whatever it was it did not give her the right to hang up on me."

"You are right she should not have done that," He said.

My first thought was that he said it to shut me up. He grabbed my hand to reassure me that everything was going to work out okay. We finished our lunch and headed to the car to go home. I noticed a help wanted sign and made a mental note to let Shonda know that they were hiring. Her oldest son should be working age. Shonda was the only one that seemed to be on my side when it came to the choir. I didn't know much about her, but I did know that she was a friendly face during practice.

I honestly dreaded having to go back to another Hot Mess practice, but I tried to keep in mind my husband's encouraging words. As the week passed, my days were filled with the other arrangements for the Pastor's celebration. Guest pastors had to be confirmed. Arrangements for the hotels and transportation needed to be made. This was sure to be a wonderful celebration of unity.

Regardless of what the choir felt the celebration is not about the Pastor. My husband wanted to honor the tradition and bring unity to the church. He felt that the day he was announced Pastor was the first and last day he saw the church act like one. So, he decided to celebrate his day as a Unity Day.

Since the day after his installment, there has been fighting among members in leadership. Discord has trickled down to the members. Now members don't hug like they use to or speak. I honestly cannot pinpoint what happened, but I know it had something to do with the older members dying. The two Elders and the 7 members of the Senior Choir are the only older members left. Most of them are a joy to be around and are very reasonable. However, then there is Mother Odell and she is not reasonable nor a joy to be around.

Chapter 10

Shonda

I woke to the sound of cereal clinking in bowls. My neck and my back ached admittedly. I looked around half sleep still and noticed that I had fallen asleep on the couch waiting for Blake to come home. For a moment I remembered waiting up for his dad to do the same thing. Disgusted, I had to remind myself that Blake was not his no-good father.

I greeted the boys as I walked toward the back of the house. Walking past Blake's room, he shared with his brothers, I noticed his bed was in the same disheveled state it was in the day before. I was certain that he came home late. I was wrong.

"Have you seen your brother" I questioned the boys. They answered no and went back to eating.

My chest began to tighten, and my breathing became labored. We live in times of little black boys not making it home. I quickly turned on the news to see if by chance he was on television. Too often I wondered how mothers felt seeing their children's picture on the news for a crime or even worse as a victim. Thank God he had not made the news.

"Mama, we going to choir today?" Byron asked

"Yes baby, but first I got to find your brother."

He walked away with his head down. Blake's actions had taken a toll on the family. It was very hard for me to devote attention to the other boys when Blake required so much time and energy.

I decided to take a shower and get dressed so that I could face what I was sure to be a horrid day. I quickly showered and dressed so that I could begin making phone calls. My first call was to Blake's best friend, who said he had not seen Blake since midnight. Midnight was Blake's curfew. The young man could not give me any information as to where Blake might have been. I called several more friends and no one had any information. I held the phone close to my chest and said a prayer. The only call left to make was to the police department. This was a call I dreaded making. My heart sank to the pit of my stomach as I dialed the first number.

Before I could get to the second number the front door open and Blake walked in my home. I was so upset and relieved I threw the phone at him. Luckily for his sake, he caught the phone before it hit him in the head.

"Ma. What are you doing?" He questioned as if he did not just come in the house at wearing yesterday's clothes.

"What am I doing? What are you doing coming in the next day? Where have you been Blake?" I yelled. The other boys quickly scurried off to their rooms. It was just me and Blake at a standoff.

I looked at him with great disappointment. I was not disappointed with him as much as I was disappointed in myself. No matter how hard I had tried I still raised a man just like his father. Tears begin to fill my eyes. He came close to comfort me, but I pushed him away. There was nothing he could say. Nothing would make up for him being out all night.

"You haven't answered me, where were you?" I said in a soft tone that scared me. I was very calm unusually calm.

"I was just out I had to think."

"You had to think," I repeated this time even more calmly.

Everything in me wanted to go off. I wanted to beat him, yell and ban him from leaving the house. I wanted to kick and throw things. How could he stand there and justify his being out all night with I had to think? I thought to myself, what did my sixteen-year-old have to think about that had him out all night. Lord he done got somebody's child pregnant.

"Okay what is her name and how far along is she?" I ask with my hands on my hips, bracing myself to hear the worst.

"What? No, I don't have any kids on the way, mom. I was thinking about ways to make money for us and time got away from me. I fell asleep in the car I swear." He said but his eyes told a different story.

I knew he was lying. Just like his father, his eyes always widen when he was lying. He was up to something I just could not put my finger on it. Something was not right, I was determined to figure out what it was and fix it! My child's life was worth much more than a couple of dollars.

"Go get ready for choir," I said in my calm voice.

"What, naw ma! I'm tired, I can't today."

"Thought you fell asleep in the car?" I said looking him up and down. "Go get ready now!" This time my voice was not calm, and I heard the other boys scurry to get dressed as well.

I did not say a word the entire ride to church. I just talked to the Lord in my head. I could not understand how I could work so hard yet feel so much hardship. I wondered if I was being punished for my past. Is all this pain because the boys have different fathers and I searched for love in all the wrong places before finding Jesus? I wondered if this was some sort of a sick test to see if I would revert to my old ways, find a man to be in the boy's lives. Well if that was what Satan was waiting for he would have a very long wait! No matter what goes on I know that God will work it out. I am not sure how He is going to straighten Blake out but Lord whatever you need to do, please do!

Chapter 11

Donnell

I woke up with a big smile. I had the best dream I have had in a long time. In my dream, Stacey and I were getting married and Eva was the flower girl. She was so beautiful in her little soft pink dress. Then the dream switched, and we were all together laughing and watching a movie, Stacey, Eva and I. God had given me the desires of my heart and I was blessed.

I looked at my phone and saw that Stacey had not returned my call or sent a text that she got my message. Although I was discouraged, I was also determined to keep a hopeful spirit. God did reveal in a dream after all my happy ending.

I made my way to the shower thinking of my dream and how wonderful it would be to have Eva and Stacey here. I try not to hate Tiffany but seeing the condition she has my child living in made it very hard.

My poor baby looked like no one has cared for her. Only God knows when the last time her hair was combed before I did it last night. I can't help but think that maybe I should have given her a bath before I put her to bed. Only God knows when the last time she had one of those. She did not smell so I figured she was okay. I prayed that her mother would at least wash her up if not give her a bath this morning.

After my bath, I quickly ate breakfast and headed to choir practice. I got there just as Stacey was walking toward the church. Admiring her modesty and beauty I almost hit a parked car.

"Come on D, you got to get this girl off your mind," I said as I pulled in properly to the parking spot.

As I slowly walked into the choir room my eyes met with Stacey's. This time she did not turn away, instead, she smiled.

"OMG, she smiled," I whispered to myself.

I casually walked over to her and said hello. She smiled again and said hello back.

"I called you," I said

"I know I was out and it was late by the time I returned home."

"Oh, I see you were on a date. Lucky dude."

"You are so silly, I was not on a date. The last man I dated broke my heart."

"Really how?"

"He got another woman pregnant." She said.

I thought I was going to die right there in the church. I was that dude that broke her heart. But then it came to me she said the last dude she dated. I was the last one. She had not dated anyone since we broke up. I held in my grin. I was the last man she loved.

"Can we talk right after practice?" I asked praying that she would say yes. She nodded, and I moved to my section as practice begun.

The Hot Mess Choir sounded flat. We were making a noise, but it was not joyful. Lady D stood in front of us trying to get the will of God out of our voices. It appeared that the more she tried, the worse it got. The senior members were singing on one key and the children were on another. The adults and the young adults kept bumping into each other as they swayed to the music. Lady D finally asked everyone to take a break. I could tell she was in the corner praying.

"Hey Stacey," I said "can I ask your forgiveness. It occurred to me that in all this time of saying how sorry I am, I never asked you to forgive me. I have already asked God and He has forgiven me. But it would mean everything if you would consider forgiveness."

"I have already forgiven you, I had to for me." She said as her eyes peered through mine.

Before I could say another word, we were called back to practice. Whatever Lady D prayed worked because the choir stopped bumping into one another. But her prayer did not fix the noise that was the choir. The choir sounded like a roomful of competing voices. We got through one song and switched to another. The second song was a favorite of all the choirs, which is probably why she chose it for us to sing. We did an amazing job butchering everyone's favorite song.

Lady D hung her head as if she could not believe what she just heard. I, on the other hand, prayed that this was the last song so that I could speak to Stacey. I was grateful when I heard Lady D say that will be all for today. I took Stacey's hand and led her outside while Mother Odell was trying to get everyone to listen to her announcement.

"So, will you?"

"Will I what?"

"Forgive me."

"I told you I already did."

"Then why are you so cold to me?"

"What do you mean I speak."

"Stacey let me take you to lunch," I said breaking the back and forth conversation. She stood quietly for a moment before smiling.

"Okay."

I walked her to my car and opened the door for her. She smelled like heaven and I was excited that she agreed. I looked up at the sky and thanked the Lord before getting into the car.

During our time together, we laughed like old friends. She let me order for her at the restaurant. She looked shocked that I remembered her favorite meal. I was unsure why she was shocked. I remembered everything about her. We talked for hours in the restaurant about everything from the choir to our jobs. I could not help but smile as she spoke. Next, to Eva, this girl was the light of my world. As our lunch date ended we vowed to keep in contact more and although it was not what I wanted, it was a step in the right direction.

Chapter 12

Mother Odell

As soon as practice ended I knew I had to take control of the room. It wasn't like Miss First Lady had any control. The choir sounded worse than it did during our first practice.

I gathered everyone except that fast Sister Stacey and that smooth operator Brother Donnell. They snuck out before I got complete control of the room. After gathering everyone, I told them to all have a seat. Miss Thing, Miss First Lady looked shocked, but she took a seat too.

"Protocol dictates that we have a meeting of the choir before we go to the elders and church pastor. I exercise my right as a tithe paying, born again, fire baptized, Mother of Holy Missionary Church to call a meeting to talk about disbanding the Hot Mess, I mean Holy Mass Choir." I said as I looked around to see if anyone dared to disagree with me.

The whole room was silent. Most choir members just sat with their mouths hanging open. They stared at me as if I had said something strange. What I said was not strange at all, in fact, if the members were honest they would agree. Miss First Lady sat in the front row rubbing her temples. I hope she did not think that fazed me because it did not! You got to get up mighty early to faze this old bird.

"Mother Odell" First Lady Deidra began "on what grounds do you want to end the choirs?"

"Oh, no honey not the choirs, this choir! The other choirs are perfectly okay singing on their Sunday and the Senior Choir can sing for this celebration foolishness your husband has cooked up. I think we should take a vote."

"No, we should not Mother Odell, you still have not expressed your reason for not wanting the choir to sing."

I stared at her, no this little girl didn't try to come at me with protocol. She must not fully understand who I am!

"On the grounds that it has never been done before and is not aligned with the traditions of the church."

"With all due respect Mother Odell, Psalm 33:3 says Sing unto him a new song: play skillfully with a loud noise."

Did this little girl just quote the Bible to me? The King James version of the Bible, she is quoting to me!

"Yes, keyword being skillful. We are not skillful we are making noise!"

"Again, Mother Odell, the Word tells us to make a joyful noise unto the Lord. It is not about the sound this is not a concert. It is about praising no matter what life is throwing at you. There is power in our praise. I know we sound a little rough now but when we all come on one accord and agree we will be just fine. I honestly see no reason to disband the choir. It is our way of showing that we are one body with many members. Now I am not holding anyone hostage, anyone is free to leave. I hope, however, that all of you will stay. Even you Mother Odell."

"Even me." I laughed. This little girl just doesn't know I already have three-fourths of the choir on my side. I am not sure just who she thinks she is playing with.

I look over towards the members that were at my house and notice that some of them are not making eye contact with me. Those turncoats are probably switching sides. I don't know why. Just because Miss Thing can quote scripture, that does not mean a hill of beans to me. The Devil himself knew the Word. I take a hard look at the members of the Senior Choir hoping one of them would stand up and say something. No one said anything. For the next thirty minutes, Miss Thing and I went back and forth. We traded scripture after scripture concerning the choir. The members just sat there like this was a tennis match. Their heads swayed back and forth as we spoke. In the end, I knew that I was going to be victorious.

"Well we could do this all day, but what will end this now is a vote. I think we should vote to see if we should bring this matter before the leaders of the church. You and I can stand and talk all day, but at the end of the day, it is the vision of the leadership that must go forth. I am more than sure they do not want to see a hot mess." I said as she stood and faced the choir.

She called for a vote on taking the matter to leadership. I knew that most of the members would vote with me. I was wrong! Only three people other than me raised their hands. She called for a vote on disbanding the choir and again. I and three others were the only ones to raise our hands. I was appalled. These traders sat up in my house, ate all my food and had the nerve to side with this girl! I stared at them with vengeance on my mind. They would pay for making me look foolish in front of everyone.

"Seeing that no one wants to take this matter to leadership and everyone is staying I think we can end this now. However, if anyone has anything to say please do so at this time." She said in her sweet irritating voice.

"Well, First Lady D I would like to say I think you are doing a great job. I know that we are a tough group to work with, but you are doing good. You keep it up and do not give up on us. We will get it together after a while." That old snake Brother Johnson said.

I gave the room full of traders one cold stare. Then I grabbed my purse and left the choir room. Just like Jesus in the garden, I was betrayed, but just like Jesus, I was determined to rise again.

Chapter 13

Deidra

I sat against the hard chair in disbelief. The choir members left one by one, some of them stopping to tell me goodbye or place their hand on mine. Most of the left looking like I felt, shocked. For what felt like an eternity, I went back and forth with Mother Odell. I am sure she did not expect me to know the Word as I did. Not only did she accuse me of horrible things she found scripture to back up her claim. I sat in that hard chair determined not to cry. I was so mad that my nose began to run. Reaching in my bag for a tissue I noticed I missed a phone call from Sheila. I could not wait to give her a call. I gathered my things and headed to my car. I could not say all that I was going to say in the church.

Sheila was my best friend. She believed in the Lord, but she would be the first to tell you God was not done with her yet. I got in my car and made sure to take the call off the Bluetooth. I did not want to risk passersby hearing my conversation. I also did not want to risk them hearing the colorful commentary Sheila was sure to give once she found out about practice today.

"Hey Boo, I did not want anything was just checking on you. As ya'll church folks would say, you were in my spirit." She said as soon as she answered the phone.

"Girl!" I said.

"Oh no, something has happened. I knew it. I knew it. Girl what done happen now."

I told her about Mother Odell and all the voting and protocol stuff. I was trying to keep from crying but as I relived the moment the tears began to fall. I never thought I would have to speak to an elder in that manner. I, unfortunately, had no choice. It felt like the nicer I was, the harder she came for my throat. I felt as if I was trapped in a corner and the only weapon I had was the word of God. So, I used the most powerful weapon I owned. Sure, she had the word as well, but I had truth on my side.

Sheila being a good friend listened to me mumble through the tears and tell her every sordid detail of my day. Then like any true ride or die, friend, she went off. She spoke in her most colorful unholy language loudly. I had to pull the phone from my ear a couple of times because she was so loud.

"Lord, this woman is going to make me come to church!" She shouted through the cell phone. "I am going to get arrested at church, Lord bless my soul. Ya'll going to have to take up an offering to bail me out. Have mercy, Jesus!"

I could not help but laugh at my silly friend. Although I laughed I was slightly nervous because I could not know for sure if she was serious. It would not have been her first time getting arrested for assault.

"You laughing, I am dead serious Dee. This woman needs to be put in her place and I am not talking about with no scriptures."

"We battle not against flesh and blood," I whispered

"Yea well we are going to see some flesh and some blood, let her keep on!"

I could not help but laugh again. Maybe Sheila's purpose in my life was to make me smile because God knows I cannot let her anywhere near Mother Odell.

After I thanked Sheila for her love and concern I pulled out of the church parking lot. I drove home in complete silence. I normally would listen to some gospel or one of my husband's sermons in times like these but not this time. I needed peace, so I took the long way home hoping that God would speak in the stillness and quiet.

When I arrived home, Myron had hot tea ready for me. He had it sitting near the couch and he met me at the door to take my purse and other belongings. As I flopped on the couch he took off my shoes and gave me a reassuring smile. I began to worry. One of the members must have called him and told him about the horrible mess I made at today's practice.

"So, it was rough today?" He questioned I just nodded my head. "It will be okay. As I understand it you handle yourself very well, I am proud of you."

"Lord, one of the members called you, didn't they!" I said embarrassed.

"No, actually Sheila called and gave me an ear full. Lord, we got to get her saved for real. I did not know she could cuss like that! Anyway, after I explained that I would be the only one laying hands at the church she explained how you handled things. I think you did well. Mother is one of those traditional seasoned saints not too many people can hang with. You did! That is wonderful, and you did not compromise your position or your walk as a woman of God. I am sure it was tough, but I am so proud of you." He said as he wrapped his bear-like arms around me.

I felt better in his embrace. Being in his arms recharged me. We sat and talked about the upcoming celebration. Today was proof that it was necessary to have a celebration of unity. My only concern is getting the choir to sing with one unified voice.

Chapter 14

Shonda

Talk about a hot mess! I have never in all my life seen church folk act like that. I thought Lady D was going to come unglued. I was so impressed by her actions. I would have totally cuss Mother Odell out, but not my First Lady she handled it with dignity. She did not let Mother Odell see her sweat, she did not elevate her voice or get out of character. With ease and the Word of God, she put Mother Odell in her proper place, took a vote, and won! She was my hero. I needed to use some of those tactics with the boys. I find myself wanting to cuss often, especially with Blake. He is turning into my worst nightmare. He talks back, comes in late and is becoming a bad example for the other boys.

Right now, he was listening to God knows what on his phone with his earphones plugged in. The other boys are occupied as I drive home from choir practice. I need to have a talk with Blake, but I am unsure how it is going to go considering his attitude.

As I unload the car of busy boys I ask Blake to watch his brothers while I go to the store. His look said it all. His face is turned up and he looked as if I am ruining his plans. I repeated myself for his clarity.

"I heard you! Dang! I know you don't have to say it again, keep my eye on your kids. I got it!" He yelled.

If I were my momma, he would be on the floor picking up his teeth. How dare he speak to me that way? I remember what happened today and try to use Lady D's strategy.

"Young man, the last I checked you were my child, not my man. You will not speak to me in that tone and you will do everything I say no matter how many times I say it." I said as he stared at me.

"Man. Whatever." He said as he walked in the house.

I sat in the car for a moment biting my bottom lip. Should I jump out the car and kill him? Should I ban him from going out? What do you do with a growing boy, that is as my momma would say, smelling himself?

I loved going to the grocery store alone. Although the boys are helpful, I can think clearly when they are not with me. Having only a few dollars I find a way to stretch my money and create a menu for the next couple of days. Tonight will be chicken and noodles, tomorrow pasta, and lastly rice with beans. Three days on a couple bucks has me feeling accomplished. I know it is not gourmet, but it is dinner and the boys will have full stomachs.

As I stumbled into the house with the grocery bags I notice that the house is a mess again. I am not sure what has gone on, but stuff is everywhere. I was only gone for a couple of hours and you would think that I left them alone for a weekend.

"Boys can ya'll pick up this house and help with the grocery bags please!" I yell. All the boys except for Blake get up and scurry to help in some sort of way.

I roll my eyes as I walk past Blake, who is sitting on the couch playing his game. In no mood to fight, I go to the kitchen and put the food in the cabinets. After the food is put away I start with the household chores. I feel like Snow White with six dwarfs instead of seven.

"Can I go out later tonight?" Blake said as he briefly looked up from the television.

"No, you don't know when to come home, so I think you should stay in a while," I said as I dusted the table near him.

"Man whatever," he mumbled, "Aye, what are you cooking for dinner." He said with an unusually stern voice.

I look at him as if he has two heads, this boy has become too much. "Chicken and noodles," I said as I bit my bottom lip.

"Naw man, I told you last time you cooked that I did not like that. You stay doing that! Why you going to make something no one likes to eat. You don't make any sense!"

I took a much-needed deep breath "I can only cook what I can afford sir." I said trying not to let my blood pressure get elevated. "It is all that I have so that is what is for dinner. You can eat it or you can eat nothing, it is up to you."

"I'll be,"

"You'll be what?" I stopped him before he had the chance to cuss in my house.

"Man, whatever." He said as he got up and walked out the door.

I ran after him, but he just kept going. Frustration prevented me from following him down the street. I went inside and with tears in my eyes, I finished my housework as the other boys played.

"Mama, where is Blake?" Bradley asked as he played with his bowl of chicken and noodles. No one wanted to eat chicken and noodles, not even me. However, chicken and noodles were what we had to eat.

"I am not sure baby, stop playing with your food and eat," I said as worry consumed my appetite.

One part of my heart was upset with Blake for leaving, the other part was scared that something could have happened to him. After I put the boys to bed, I called a couple of Blake's friends. None of the friends I called knew where Blake was. They all said they had not spoken with him in some time. This worried me even more. Blake was not hanging out with his normal crowd. I was unsure of what type of people my son was involved with or what he had been doing all night.

Just as I begin to pray my phone rang.

"Mom it's Blake. I am in jail, come get me please." Was all I heard.

Chapter 15

Donnell

I must be honest I am a little hesitant about today's choir practice. My homeboy told me about all of the wicked stuff that went on in the last practice. I heard that Lady D handled herself well against Mother Odell. Mother Odell is too old to be starting foolishness in the church. I wonder if bringing Eva will be a good idea.

I am blessed to have her this weekend and to have the weekend off from work. I planned to take my sweetie pie to choir practice and then to the park. The weather is mild, so I lay out some cute jeans and a top the same color as mine. I found her baby Air Force 1's before I wake her up. I can't help myself from watching her sleep. She is so peaceful breathing in and out curled up in a little ball. I shake her gently and she turns to me and smiles.

I am well aware of the fact that she was conceived out of my sin, but she is a blessing to me. I brush her little teeth and get her dressed for our day. I wish that I could do this every day not just on weekends when her mother felt fed up with child rearing. We hopped into my car after breakfast and head toward the church.

As soon as we pulled up I hear the oohs from the ladies and little girls at church.

"Oh my God, she is so cute."

"Aw look they match down to their shoes."

"Look at her she is too cute, with her daddy."

"That's what I am talking about, that man takes care of his."

I'd be lying if I said the comments did not make me feel good. It is very rare that a black man gets props for taking care of his kids. So much of media is filled with deadbeat dads not caring, it is great to be recognized for doing what is right. As we get closer to the church I see Stacey standing by the door. She is the most beautiful woman in the world next to my Eva of course. Her natural hair blows slightly in the mild wind and I catch the smell of her perfume as I get closer.

"Wow look who is here. She is so cute Donnell." Stacey said as she bent down to speak to Eva. "Hi princess, are you coming to sing today?" She asked the shy Eva who holds my hand tightly.

"Don't be scared, Miss Stacey is a nice lady," I told Eva.

"Up," Eva said holding her hands up in the air so that I could pick her up.

As I pick her up I notice how cute we look walking into the church. Eva in my arms and Stacey by my side, we look like the perfect Christian family. I go to my section of the choir room and stand Eva in front of me.

Eva is well behaved during the practice, she even tried to sing some of the songs. The practice is still not as smooth as young adult practice. Members are still trying to out-sing one another. Loud is not always correct I think to myself as I looked over at some of the members. I would think that after the vote to stay people would be getting along better but that is not the case. Our breaks looked like a game of four corners. As soon as Lady D calls for a break each of the choirs go to their separate corners of the room.

To be a bit rebellious, I and a couple other members stand in the middle of the room. Most of the conversation is about Eva. People wanted to know everything about her. If she is in school? How old she is? Even one girl flirtatiously asked if I was still with Eva's mama. I had to take a deep breath on that only to keep from saying some ungodly words in the house of the Lord.

After practice, I asked Stacey if she would like to go to the park with Eva and me. I was surprised that she said yes and that she would meet us there. The whole entire ride to the park I talk to Eva about my excitement. Eva, who had no idea of what I was talking about, just smiled. I prayed to God that this would be the start of something wonderful, that Stacey would fall in love with Eva and with me.

Once at the park, we took turns pushing Eva in the swing. We raced up the hill and down again and again. Eva's laugh was so contagious we found ourselves laughing for no reason. Stacey helped Eva walk up the stairs to the slide and I waited at the bottom to catch her as she slid down. Stacey held Eva's hand and they ran from one play structure to the next. I was in love. We finally decided to let Eva play in the sandbox while we sat nearby to chat.

Our conversation was basic. It was filled with long pauses and us staring deeply into each other's eyes. Then, we would turn away and giggle softly. Eva played quietly in the sand. I wanted to tell Stacey so much, but I did not know where to start or what to say. I watched the wind blow through her natural hair and inhaled her sweet perfume. She was everything I wanted in a wife. She loved the Lord, had a good head on her shoulders and based on today I knew she could love Eva.

As she turned to face me I could not help myself, I kissed her. To my surprise, she kissed me back. We smiled at one another and held hands as we finished watching Eva play.

Chapter 16

Mother Odell

I'm not certain what Miss Thing thought she was doing today at choir practice. She seemed to at one point have it together but as always it was a hot mess. I'm not sure how but God willing I will put an end to this foolishness one way or another.

The church leadership meeting starts an hour after practice, so I think it is best I stick around the church. I went into the church with my Bible to have some prayer and quiet time with my Jesus before the meeting. Just as I enter the church guess who I see? None other than Miss Thing herself sitting in the back of the church with her head down. She would be sitting in the back.

I sat on the second row where I sat every Sunday and pulled out my Bible. I was going to need some scripture references for this meeting. I am not sure what the Pastor and the other leaders are thinking but this foolishness is unholy and needs to stop.

I spent the next hour reading my Word and talking to my Lord. Certainly, He must have a plan. Just as the meeting is about to start I make my way to the office conference room.

To my dismay and surprise, Miss Thing was sitting at the conference table next to her husband the Pastor. I rolled my eyes, walk into the room and take my seat.

"Well, what is this why is she here, I thought this was a leadership meeting?" I questioned

"This is, and Mother Odell she is the First Lady of this church which places her in leadership. She is also over a major program and I trust you will give FIRST Lady Deidra your respect." Pastor Jones said.

I looked at him and nodded with my lips perched. I will respect her alright. The meeting started as all these meetings do with prayer and reports. I tried to stare a hole in First Lady Deidra's forehead, but it did not work. No matter how I looked at her or what I said she seemed to be unbothered. I scoffed during her report, yet she still seemed unfazed. I questioned her progress and she answered with a smile.

No matter what I seem to throw at her she had something to say that was pleasant. The more I tried the smoother she became. She dodged my attacks like a professional dodgeball player. I wasn't done yet, however.

I know church folk and I know leadership and when you want to see them squirm there is only one point you need to bring to the table. Money! The thought of paying for, budgeting for or fundraising for any event will turn a committee upside down. Holy Missionary Baptist Church was no different than any other black church we are always in need of an extra dollar. Which meant we did not have the money to pay for a fancy program. There was no room in the budget. I would know because I help with the finances twice a month.

"Brother Pastor," I began real sweet, "With all due respect to your vision. I do not see how we can pull off such an elaborate affair with our small budget. We do not have funds to house guest speakers nor do we have money to entertain the thought of gifts. I think that this celebration should be tabled to a time when we are in a better position to have an affair such as this. Furthermore, in my 45 years of being at this very church, we have never celebrated or lifted any man above Jesus. So, to celebrate you after only a year. I mean our last Pastor built this very room and we did not celebrate him we celebrated Jesus. No disrespect Pastor we love you, I just think well, we just think this is not the time nor the place for such a thing." I said looking around for someone to agree with me. Not one of those cowards in the room agreed!

"Mother Odell, maybe there is some miscommunication about the celebration. Yes, it is my anniversary, but I am having a celebration of church unity. This is not a party for me. I want to help bring the church back together. That is why I asked my wife to form the Holy Mass Choir. On that note as leadership, I would hope that no one in this room is referring to the Mass Choir as the Hot Mess Choir. I would be very upset to know that leadership does not share the vision of unity." He said as he looked around.

I just stared at him and nodded. He is young, and he has to learn. You do not mess with tradition. The roots of this church run deep, and they are deep for a reason. How dare he not be here a whole year and say that we are not unified. He is not unified. Sure, we have our issues, but we come together if need be. He certainly has no idea what he is doing as Pastor, and it makes me wonder if he and his wife should leave. I make a mental note to speak to the head deacon.

Willie has been sweet on me since the passing of my husband. I just will not give him the time of day. One reason is I'm still in love with my husband, God bless the dead and the other is it would be too strange, both our names being Willie. None the less, I planned to cozy up to Deacon Willie, so he can help me take down the Pastor and his wife. After the meeting, I ask the deacon if he would walk me to my car. He said yes of course and that gave me the perfect opportunity to ask him to coffee so that we can talk.

Chapter 17

Deidra

No matter how hard I pray the week seems to fly by. It felt like it was just Monday when I went to sleep. Now it is Saturday morning and I must face the Hot Mess Choir once again. As always, my husband is sleeping like a bear next to me. How he can remain so peaceful during this time I do not understand.

Mother Odell did everything in her power to stop anything we were trying to do at the church last weekend. She has it out for us and I wish I could understand why. Ever since the day of my husband's installment as Pastor she has tried to the throw a wrench in the plans. She is evil. I close my eyes and say a short prayer before getting out of bed.

Working on this project has been such a struggle. The choirs on their own sound wonderful. They would easily bring a tear to your eye and usher you into worship. But God bless them, together they are a hot mess. I have seniors trying to out -sing everybody, children trying to find some sort of direction and adults arguing over leads. I never said we were singing songs with leads!

I take a quick shower and have my quiet time with the Lord. I prayed that somehow today's practice is better than the ones that we have had in the past. I chose to put on pants again because I wanted to prove to Mother Odell that she does not run me or anything else at Holy Missionary Baptist Church.

Once I arrived at the church I stopped in the sanctuary to pray again. I figure it would not hurt to make sure I was completely covered. Today we were singing new songs and as my mama would say, new level new devil.

Everyone was on time to practice except Mother Odell. Which I can say pleased me to be able to get through a new song without her.

"I'm so sorry I am late." She said loudly as if anyone cared. Honestly, I thought the practice was going well without her. "You know the devil is busy." She continued. "But he ain't gonna win!" She said, and she looked right at me.

How dare she? She really has some balls under that long ugly dress. She took her place in the choir room and began to look over the shoulder of a member for the words. I reluctantly handed her a copy. She began to sing loud, off-key and out of tune.

"Lord have mercy," I whispered

"Excuse me? Did you say something dear?" Mother Odell said staring at me.

"I was talking to the Lord, not you," I said tired of playing nice.

"You need to!"

"What is that supposed to mean?"

"Just what I said, you need to! You desperately need to seek His face. Because you are totally out of order!"

I placed my hand on my hip, cocked my head to the side and prepared to give Mother Willie Mae Odell the business she was so deserving of.

"Lady D don't let the devil get you out of character," A choir member said.

"Yea Lady D let's just finish practice."

"Yea, we were sounding good." Another member said.

I gathered myself and started the song over. Everyone including Mother Odell sang. The members were right they did sound much better singing this new song. Everyone was on one accord, even the children. I had to admit I was a little worried when I introduced the song to the choir. I did not tell them that it was one of the Pastor's favorite songs because I wanted it to be a surprise when we sang.

I was the one surprised by the choir. Each of them sang their parts on key and together. It was a popular song that I guess they could identify with on some level. I was just grateful that they could sing the song.

During our break, I wondered if I should say something to Mother Odell. Her antics were getting out of hand and that was no way to act in front of children and new believers. They would not understand her actions and might think that her behavior was true for all Christians. Just as I went to approach her Shonda stopped me.

"First Lady could you pray for my son." She said.

"I had to pick him up from the jail the other day."

"Oh my God sis, is he okay?" I questioned.

"Yes. I just don't know what to do. He is a good kid normally. Lately, he has been with the wrong crowd a different crowd. I would have brought the boys today, but I just needed some time with God alone."

"No, I understand and yes I will pray."

We went back to practice, but I could not stop thinking about Shonda and her sons. Every practice and every church service she would have her boys in the house of the Lord. My God that poor girl must be torn up was all I could think, and Mother Odell is playing childhood games when people have real problems.

I had to check myself again because I saw my anger rise. My face felt hot and I could not take my eyes off Mother Odell. I finally regained my composure long enough to lead the choir in the final song for the practice. They amazed me again. They sang the next song better than they sang the first. I felt tears of joy come to my eyes.

This is what I had been praying for all day. They were finally coming together. Not even evil Mother Odell could say otherwise. She looked around as she sang. She appeared to be shocked by the togetherness in everyone's voices. Someone nudged her to get her back on focus. With one voice the Hot Mess Choir sang the final song of practice.

"Guys remember we have testimony service in the morning I hope to see you all there," I said with a smile as we ended the practice.

Chapter 18

Shonda

The one thing that I loved about Holy Missionary's new vision is the testimony services. We did not have these types of services during the reign of our old pastor. This was an old idea brought to light by Pastor Myron. When I was young my grandmother would have testimony service at her church. She would say they were reminders that God could do anything and that the devil wanted us to sit back and not tell people our troubles so that we could be trapped. I was unsure if I was going to say anything during the service. In my gut, I wanted to but more importantly, I no longer wanted to be trapped.

For the past couple of months, I had felt trapped by my kids and my responsibility as their mother. Being a single parent is tough work and having six boys makes it harder than I could ever imagine. The younger boys are growing out of their clothes, the twins are going through a weird phase and God only knows what I am to do with Blake.

I decided to leave the boys home and go to service by myself. I was still in need of some time alone with God. I did not feel like threatening the boys to behave or dealing with Blakes noncompliance. So, I left them with plenty of food and entertainment and headed to church.

I have to be honest it felt good walking in the church and sitting down without having to worry if the boys were talking, playing or not paying attention. I did not have to take anybody's phone or tablet. I did not have to look at sulking faces, nor did I have to intercept notes from fast girls looking at the boys. I smiled to myself as I cozied in my seat.

Service started with worship. I enjoyed worshiping the Father. The song told of His mercy and grace. I was in need of both mercy and grace. Tears began to fall from my eyes as I worshipped. I felt the usher put a tissue in my hand as I worshipped. After drying my eyes, I could feel the presence of the Holy Spirit. It ran over my body like a cool calming breeze. Little chill bumps appeared on my arm out of nowhere. I began to cry again as I was blanketed in the love of Christ.

So many things had taken place in a short time. Blake was out of jail and although no charges were to be filed, the fact that I had to pick him up from that place gave my heart so much pain. Our relationship had been changed forever. I once thought the other boys would look up to him. Now, I prayed they did the opposite of anything Blake did.

After worship Pastor had a couple of words to say. He basically gave a nice version of the rules of testimony service and the background. I chuckled at the twisted look on Mother Odell's face when Pastor Myron gave the history. I am sure he threw the history part of the service in for her. She is always one to have something bad to say about everything the church does. Once the ground rules were set people began to make a line to testify. The testimonies were so uplifting. I was encouraged by the young couple that told of how they prayed and waited for God to give them a child. They were excited to announce that they were having a baby. The church broke out in praise for their blessing.

The couple's struggle reminded me that if God could answer their prayer He could answer mine. There was a man that struggled with his business and he was seeking prayer. He said he was coming up to pre-testify. I liked the sound of testifying before it happened as a way to activate your faith. I pre-testified from my seat.

As I sat there something in my spirit nudged me. I remembered my grandmother's teaching. Sometimes we go through things for others so that we can be a light in a dark world. Even the things we bring on ourselves can help others. I felt the nudge again. I sat up in my seat. My feet and legs began to stand me up reluctantly. I was nervous all of a sudden, my heart beat heavily in my chest and I was sweating a little. I made my way to the line and tried not to make eye contact with anyone. I went over the speaking protocol in my head as I inched closer in line toward the front. I took a deep breath and walk to the microphone when it was my turn to speak.

"Giving honor to God who is the head of my life, Pastor and those in leadership, God has been good." I started. "A few days ago, I guess, I don't know time goes so fast lately, I had to pick my son up from jail. It was not his fault, and everything is ok, but it could have been so different. I want to thank First Lady Deidra for calling and praying with me. She really stood by my side. I come to do like the one gentleman and pre- testify. I don't know how God is going to do it and honestly, that ain't none of my business, but I know He will. I come to tell y'all that my son is going to love the Lord, be respectful and helpful. His life is going to change. I can say this because the Bible says that I can have the desires of my heart. Well church, my heart desire is that my son's life change. I stand here today to tell you that it will happen." As the tears streamed down my face I slowly walked to my seat. Some of the members looked at me with judgment in their eyes, others praised Jesus for me and with me.

Chapter 19

Donnell

I sat with my back straight against my chair. People praised and shouted to the glory of the Lord. I even found myself caught in the emotional whirlwind. Each testimony was powerful and caused people to be delivered or, so it appeared. Many of the women were crying as they thanked God for blessings unknown to the congregation.

I looked over at Stacey, who was sitting a few rows over from me. She wore a pale pink dress and cream shoes. I admired the way she always looked put together and sophisticated. Her natural hair was put up in a bun that looked like a knot on the top of her head. She wore very little makeup. I could not help but notice everything about her. She was an angel. She was a Proverbs 31 woman waiting on her Boaz to arrive.

If I had anything to say about it I would be her Boaz, her knight in shining armor and her dream come true. I had to shake myself here I was in church thinking about Stacey, not bad thoughts, to the contrary I had nothing but good thoughts and pure intentions when it came to Stacey.

The birth of Eva changed me. I no longer look at women the same, since she came into my life. I would not want a man to do her the way I have done some women in my day. I wanted nothing but the best for Eva and I plan to be nothing but the best for Stacey. My only problem was getting Stacey to see that I was serious and that I had her best interest in my mind. This was not going to be an easy task. Sure, we talked every day now, and we even shared one romantic kiss, but she was still guarded.

Stacey would only let me get so close then she would shut me down. It is not like I was trying to have sex with her. I would hold her hand as we walked and then after a while, she would let me go as if she had just realized what she had done. She would hug me but then back off like I had the plague. I went to the only man I trust, Pastor Myron because I wanted to make sure I was not doing anything wrong. He gave me sound advice. He said to just be honest. Honest was what I was going to be, starting now.

I got up slowly from my seat. As I stood to my feet my heart was sure of what needed to be done. My mind, however, was unsure as I walked to the line of members ready to testify. I stood behind several people that praised for the gifts that God had given them. Their gifts were nice but they did not compare to my gift. God had blessed me with an angel and I vowed to do right by my gift.

As I got closer to the front of the line I could feel my heart pound in my chest. I was nervous, but I did not care. I knew what needed to be done. After the lady in front of me testified about her blood pressure she handed me the microphone.

"Giving honor to God and the Pastor and the leaders." I began nervously. "A few years ago, I was a different person. I thought I knew it all! I had every worldly thing you could want. Sure, I went to church and did the God thing. I was not as serious as I needed to be. I was in a relationship but because I was full of myself, I thought I could have fun on the side. Well, that fun on the side resulted in a little girl being born. When I held my daughter, I realized the power of God and the power of His forgiveness. I became serious about the things of God and I repented." I said as several members shouted amen. "I am not perfect, but I am working towards it. I spoke to the Pastor the other day and he being the great mentor he is, challenged me to be completely honest with myself and my heart. So, I must honestly say in front of God and the members of this church, Stacey I love you. I would very much like it if we could work towards a future together. I know it is going to take time and I am willing to wait the allotted time." I stood heart in my hands and I looked at her.

It was as if we were the only two people in the church for a moment. She had tears streaming down her face as she shook her head yes. I was overjoyed. I thanked everyone and went to sit by my girl. We hugged tightly for a moment before we turned back towards the service. I was unsure of what God was doing but I was glad.

We sat next to each other the whole service for the first time. We praised together, and we shouted to the glory of God. One member testified that she was in need of prayer and we prayed together. I was blessed beyond measure.

The line of members wanting to testify seemed to have grown after each person spoke. They all told of the goodness of God how He delivered them and changed their hearts. I could not help but notice Mother Odell standing at the end of the line with a sinister look on her face. She rocked back and forth as she stood with her arms folded and her eyes fixed on the microphone.

Chapter 20

Mother Odell

I stood in the long line rocking back and forth. I tried to control my anger. My gaze was fixed on the microphone to keep me from looking at Deacon Willie. Ever since our chat after choir practice he had been sniffing around my skirt. I do not want him. I wanted him to come aboard my plan to take down this program the pastor and his wife cooked up.

He kept telling me how the program was going to be awesome and how God would be blessed. He like the others was wrong! How God was going to get the glory was beyond my simple mind.

I waited as person after person testified to what they thought was the goodness of the Lord. The last time I checked the Lord was not a genie He did not grant wishes. I moved up the line slowly waiting to set the record straight for the saints and the ain'ts.

My mind thought to Albert for a moment. If he was here none of this foolishness would be going on at all. He was the strongest deacon at Holy Missionary Baptist Church. He did not stand for much of this that they have going on now. As I thought of him and got closer to the microphone my eyes teared. One of the raggedy ushers gave me a tissue. I took it after I looked at her with a straight face. Some people just want to be seen.

"Go back to your post." I fussed as she swiftly went back to the back door. I shook my head. Things had been getting out of hand and I was going to set it straight.

I impatiently waited for the girl to tell the church about her healing. Then I waited for the man to tell about his car. I waited for the girl in front of me that cried all over the microphone to stop. With Jesus in my heart and lots on my mind, I took the microphone.

I stood still for a moment. I allowed those that shouted to have their time. I looked at the Pastor and his First Lady. I looked at all the cowardly leaders. I pursed my lips in disgust. These very people that sat up front where the same people that allowed foolishness and carrying on to take place in the church. They called themselves leaders, but they were followers and they followed the world's system. In the world, we lift up man and celebrate him. In the church, we lift up Jesus! Not these raggedy people they had it all twisted and followed behind a man named Myron.

"Giving honor to the most high God who is the head of my life. Who used to be the head of this church. To the Pastor, his wife, and the followers we call leaders. I must be honest as one young man said this church is going to hell. You all have allowed what you know to be right to go by the wayside. You sit up here and allow folk to testify about making love connections like this is some 80's television show. You do not have any regard for your elders, your traditions, or your foundation. My husband

Albert, God bless the dead, is probably turning in his grave as the former head of the deacon board. You all want to celebrate and decorate for man. You do not do half of that for Jesus! I said it at choir practice, but no one would hear me. I said it at the meeting, but no one would hear. So, now I am saying it in front of everybody. We don't need a Pastor celebration! We need to celebrate the Father, Son, and Holy Ghost." I said to the crowd of people that stared at me with their mouths hanging open. I stood for a moment. No one clapped or shouted they just stared at me. I did what I knew to do, I stared right back at them before taking my seat.

Someone cued the musician, who was sitting at the keyboard staring at me. He began to play a popular song for our church. Everyone began to sing and praise. I just sat there looking around at the pure foolishness that was taking place. After everything I had just said they went back to acting like they use to act.

I caught Deacon Wille looking at me out of the corner of my eye. He shook his head as if I had done something that was wrong. I did not see any wrong in what I told the people. In fact, they should consider themselves blessed I told them the truth. The truth is what sets people free.

They went on praising and singing. I went on sitting disgusted. After two worship songs and a praise song, the congregation settled down. The Pastor leaned over to his wife kissed her on her cheek and stood. He walked slowly to the pulpit. Once he was behind the pulpit he took out a tissue and wiped the sweat off his face.

I figured he was sweating because the truth is sometimes hot like the conviction of the Holy Ghost. I watched his every move. He looked at me then everyone else in the church. He took a deep breath then bowed his head. I wanted to shout speak fool, but I didn't. I let him stand and I did not say a word.

I could feel the eyes of the leaders and the want to be leaders on me. I did not care someone had to tell it like it was and that someone happen to be me at this time.

Chapter 21

Deidra

Anger burned in my chest. It is one thing to come after me, but it is a whole different story when you come at my husband. I watched Myron wipe the sweat from his face. He only did that when he was angry. He took long deep breaths that told me he was praying that God speaks for him. He stood staring at the congregation.

I sat arm folded trying to keep my peace. How dare she? For someone that was supposed to be old and seasoned in the things of the Lord, she had some nerve. She actually just got up there and told the whole church they were going to Hell. I can only take so much of her foolishness. Myron keeps reminding me that she comes from a different time period, but I still believe there was respect back in her day.

She just disrespected me and my husband. I am expected to forgive and let this go, but I do not see how I can. My heart raced as I watch my husband gather his composure. He was not one to be taken lightly when it came to matters like these.

I said a prayer for him. I did not want his anger to get the best of him and make him do something he would regret later. He stood there nodding his head as if he had just heard from the Lord. His eyes were fixed on Mother Odell. He took a deep breath and then he spoke.

"Church. The Pastor celebration is not about me. Yes, I am your Pastor and we will celebrate on my one-year anniversary, but we are not celebrating me. I am well aware of the fact that I am just a man. I am a man that loves the Lord and will lift Him up every day of the year. I am not a perfect man so as calm as I seem it is taking all of the Holy Spirit to keep me in this hour. When my wife and I came to Holy Missionary Baptist Church we were aware of your traditions. We saw and went along with many of them. However, church I can not and will not go along with a tradition that goes against the word of God. The Bible clearly states we are one body with many members.

That means that in order for us to do the will of God we must function as one body. We will have a mass choir because we are one body. We will have a unity celebration for the anniversary of me coming here as Pastor because we are one body. We will not condemn members to Hell because we are one body. The body needs all of us church, even Mother Odell. With that being said I do not want any reports of her being treated unfairly because she is part of the body.

Unity Day will be about this church coming together as one body. We will worship as one, fellowship as one, feast on the Word as one, and eat as one somebody say Amen. Church, I love y'all and I know that the Lord has big plans for us, but first, we must come together as one body." He said.

He adjusted his jacket, wiped his face and cued the band.

The band began to play one of the churches favorite hymns and everyone joined in to sing. Everyone sang even Mother Odell. After the song, a couple more people came up to testify. Their testimonies help lighten the mood and restore peace to the house of the Lord.

I was sure Mother Odell was going to have something to say to me after service because she kept looking at me out of the corner of her eye. After we were dismissed I stood up front a few steps away from my husband greeting members. Many of the members wanted me to tell Myron that they appreciated the direction that he was taking the church. Some of them said they use to feel like they were not apart of a church family. They said they would just come to church because that is what they were taught to do. One woman said it was not until we got in leadership that she felt apart of the body and she had been a member for ten years.

I thought it was so sad that so many people did not feel apart of the body. My spirit was weakened by the private testimonies that the people were sharing with me.

I thought of Mother Odell and all the fuss she was causing and wondered if maybe in some way she felt the same way these people felt. I wondered if all her hatred was just fear of being left out and alone.

Tears started to appear in my eyes as I heard member after member say how grateful they were of the direction we were taking the church. I had to excuse myself for a moment to go the restroom.

As I walked out of the restroom I saw Mother Odell. I could not say for sure that she was waiting for me, but it felt like she was waiting for me.

"Hello, Mother Odell," I said as calm as I could.

"Look, I heard what your husband said, and I just don't know. He is going about this in such a different manner. Changing things and making new things. I just don't know."

"Mother, that is understandable. But know this my husband your Pastor loves the Lord and he would not do anything that would lead people astray. So you can rest assured that we will be following Jesus in all our programming. Please know that everything we do is Bible-based."

She looked at me with her aging eyes and nodded her head. She touched my arm and walked away. I could not say for sure that she was totally on board with the vision of the church. However, God had given me a peace about the situation. I figured no matter her feelings we as a church would be okay. I walked back into the church to meet my husband so that we could get some much-needed rest.

Chapter 21

Shonda

Man talk about a hot mess, I can't believe all that went on in church. For the first time in forever, I am glad I left the boys at home. I am not sure they would be able to understand everything that took place. As I drove home I decided to stop and grab a bite to eat. I felt kind of strange because I could have sworn I saw Blake out of the corner of my eye.

I left him at home and in charge of the other boys. Although they are all old enough to stay at home by themselves, I still like having Blake in charge. He has not been the best sixteen-year-old but he is still my baby. I grab enough for myself and my tribe at home from the drive-thru.

As I pull into the driveway I noticed that the house is quiet. For a moment I paused because this seems strange. A house full of boys is never this quiet. I walked up to the door with a puzzled look on my face. I listened in and could hear the television. As I walked into the house, five of my tribe was gathered around the television set watching a movie.

"Mom!" They said excitedly. "You bought us food."

"Yes," I said looking around for my missing child. "Where is your brother?"

"Oh, he left mama, right after you did. He told us to watch a few movies and he would be back before you got home." Bradley said.

"He does it all the time mama, we know how to take care of ourselves," Bryon said in a reassuring voice.

"Yea, mama we good." Bud who was next to the oldest at 14 said."

I not knowing what to do handed out the food and went to my room. I have prayed and cried over Blake. I have praised and testified in advance over Blake. To think that he would do something like this breaks my heart. I sat on my bed with my hands in my head. I was too heartbroken to pray anymore for my son. I was in need of a break, something to ease the pain of raising this boy. I tried to reach out to his father's side of the family but got no response. I truly was his only family.

I was so upset with myself for ever getting into a situation where I had to be Blake's sole parent. Blake was one of those children that needed two parents in his life. All children need two parents, but some can make it with one. Blake was not one of these children. From birth, he was always getting into something.

I can recall always having to go to his schools for one reason or another. He started getting in trouble in preschool. Now he was almost a man and nowhere to be found. I changed my clothes and headed back to the living room. The other boys had finished up their food, cleaned up their area and were watching the end of their movie.

Just as I reached for my phone to find Blake it began to ring.

"Hello. This is she. Yes, I am the mother of Blake Williams. Oh my God. Yes. I will be right there. Yes. Do whatever you have to do. Yes. I am on my way. Bud! Keep an eye on your brothers make sure Y'all get to bed. I will be back. I am not sure when."

As I drove I was frantic. The caller was unclear about what had happened, but I was clear I needed to get there as soon as I could. I flew through several red lights and thanked God that the cops were not out. As I pulled up to the hospital I do not recall if I stopped to park or not, I flew through the emergency doors.

"Hello, I am Blake Williams' mother I got a call."

"Yes, right this way."

"Hello, I am Blake Williams' mother."

"Yes, it appears your son and his friends were in a drunk driving accident. They were hit head-on by the drunk driver at a high speed. Your son and one other passenger are the only survivors from the accident. Both drivers died at the scene of the wreck. I am so sorry that I cannot provide you with more information. Your son is still in surgery and we are doing everything we can I promise." The nurse said.

I could not breathe. I could not move. I felt as if my body floated to a nearby chair. I was unsure of what to do next. My son, my first born was clinging on to life. I contemplated calling his father's family again because the tone of the nurse voice made me think he might not make it through. I decided that if Blake did not make it I would call.

The thought of Blake not making it through this alive sent a pain throughout my body. I began to hurt all over. Out of nowhere tears poured out of my eyes like a waterfall. I bent over and began to wail. I could not comprehend life without any of my boys. I definitely could not imagine life without Blake. Sure, he was not the best kid, but he was my kid.

"Miss, can we call someone to sit with you? It is going to be a long surgery." I heard a nurse say.

I shook my head. There was no one to call but Jesus. I had been raising the boys on my own. I had no family. I was alone. Just as I was about to melt in my sorrow Pastor and First Lady came flying around the corner.

"We saw it on the news and had to come." They said.

I fell into Deidra's arms and began to cry.

Chapter 23

Donnell

I ran around the house making sure everything was in order. Feverishly, I looked for anything that was out of place. Seeing that the house was good I sat on the couch and waited. Stacey was coming over for the first time in years.

I wanted her to see that I had a nice place. I think girls like knowing their man can take care of a home. I did not have anything big planned just lunch and some movies. I rushed to the kitchen to get the meal out of the oven. This was going to be the best date we have had in a long time. I needed her to know that I was serious. Yes, I had confessed my love at church, but anybody can say the words. The true question is can they back it up with action. I loved Stacey with everything in my heart and would never hurt her again.

As I finished up in the kitchen I heard a knock on the door. I opened it to see the most beautiful creature God had created, Stacey. She wore denim jeans and a soft yellow top. Her natural hair was wild and free but still managed. She smelt like sunshine and soul music. I loved this girl.

"Hey." She said with her beautiful smile.

"Hey, you," I said as I gave her a hug.

"It smells great in here."

"Yeah, I cooked up a little something"

"Awesome, well I brought the movies."

I smiled. She was simply wonderful. I dished our food and we sat on the couch in front of the television. By the middle of the movie we had finished our food and rested our plates on the table. Stacey sat close to me and we cuddled as the movie played. I felt like a man that just walked into heaven. I had my girl back.

Without warning, there was an obnoxious bang at my front door. It startled both of us and we looked at each other. I was unsure of who it could be, the television was not up loud. I was praying it was not who I did not want it to be. My prayer went unanswered.

"Donnell! Donnell! I know you are home. I saw your car! Donnell!" the loud voice yelled.

I lowered my head and asked the Lord why before opening the door.

"What do you want?" I said partially opening the door.

"Why you peeping out your own door, you got some trick in your house."

"No, the trick is standing at the door," I said.

"Tricks and treat Bih, I need some money."

"What? You get child support what you mean you need some money."

"Don't worry about what I get and open this door. Oh, I see you got that trick Stacey up in here." She said walking past me and into the house. "Hey girl, hey. You still messing with this joker after he done had a baby on you. I swear ya'll church chicks are the worst."

I motion to Stacey not to say anything. I was hoping if we did not engage Tiffany would leave quickly.

"Tiffany, I am not giving you money when I already gave you money."

"You ain't gonna take care of Eva! That is what you are really saying.

"Look what you ain't finna do is walk in my house and tell me that I ain't taking care of my child. Where is Eva anyway?"

"At home with a real man!"

"You left my baby with one of your dudes. Woman are you crazy. Take your tail back to my baby before I get her, and you are never allowed to see her."

"Boy please that ain't never happening, trust that. So what y'all doing all boo'd up while his child is hungry, eating good I see." She said to Stacey.

"Maybe I better go so you can work this out," Stacey said as she stood up and Tiffany sat down.

"No! Baby you don't have to leave. Tiffany is not staying."

"Oh, Tiffany ain't going nowhere until she gets her some money. Did he tell you I did not even want to have Eva? Bet he did not. He begged me not to have an abortion. Said we could make it work. Bet he did not tell you that. Girl if you believe anything this liar tells you, you are more stupid then you look." Tiffany said as she looked Stacey up and down.

"Tiffany, look here is 20 dollars take it and go," I said handing her a twenty from my back pocket.

"Bih, what is twenty dollars supposed to do." She said taking the money and heading to the door.

"You can't get her this weekend, me and her stepdaddy is taking her to the theme park."

"What?" I questioned as disappointment filled my heart.

Tiffany walked out of the door and I turned to Stacey who looked as if she was about to cry.

"Stacey, you can't believe or think about anything she said. She is crazy."

"She must not have been too crazy, you made a child with her."

"Stacey, baby I love you. Please don't let my past make you forget that I love you."

"It's not your past Donnell, it is your present that I am thinking about. I am a Christian and all, but I am not going to take too many more insults and outburst from your baby mama."

"And you won't have to. I promise."

"Yea, I have dealt with your promises before Donnell."

"Stacey. Please, we can make this work I promise, I swear on everything I love."

"Donnell, I don't,"

"Stacey please, I love you and I promise I will never let you get hurt."

"Ok," Stacey said but I was unsure if she meant it.

Chapter 24

Mother Odell

It may be hard to believe, but not everyone in the church hates me. After service Miss. Thang and I had a talk and I am unsure of how I feel about her and her husband. Maggie, on the other hand, is my one true friend. Today we were going to lunch and to shop. I am grateful for the company. We planned our outing a couple days ago and I have been looking forward to going all week. I am not feeling my best but that will not stop me today.

I put on my going shopping dress and comfortable shoes. My hair is still neatly tucked in a bun, so I just smoothed the sides with a brush. I looked pretty good for an old lady. Just as I was finished up my morning routine Maggie knocked on the door.

We decided to head to lunch before we shopped. Maggie was such a good friend she, listened to me talk for hours about church and my feelings. She unlike some was not judgmental and did not take sides. She just listened. I was not feeling very well and we needed to stop halfway through our shopping trip. My body for some reason felt weak without warning. I did not know what to think as I got a little dizzy. Before we could get to the next store I began to feel a slight heaviness in my chest.

"Mother, you okay." was the last thing I heard.

I woke up in an all-white room. I could hear a faint beeping sound and see lights above my head. The lights were so bright that they caused me to blink several times.

"Aww, you're awake. You had me so scared" Maggie began, "No don't try to talk, I will go get the nurse." She finished and walked out of the door.

My body was sore all over and I could barely move. I looked around and saw that I was in the hospital. I instantly became scared because I did not understand why I was in the hospital or how I got there. The nurse walked back into the room with Maggie. The nurse did not look like she was old enough to work on me, but I was so confused I did not care.

"Ms. Willie -Mae Odell, I am Rosie I will be your nurse. You had a mild heart attack. The doctor will be in to see you shortly. How is your pain?" She asked.

"I am very sore," I said.

"Yes, that is to be expected. The doctor has ordered something, and I will give it to you now." She said with a smile.

"Thank you," I said.

After the medicine began to work I was able to talk to Maggie. She explained to me that as we shopped I began to get ill. After a while, according to Maggie, I passed out. She said the EMT was able to get to me in a hurry. Once at the hospital, the doctors worked swiftly. According to Maggie, the doctor said that I was going to be okay. I thanked God.

The doctor came into the room and confirmed what Maggie said. He told me that with some lifestyle changes I would be okay after recovery. I thanked God again. God had spared my life. Although I love the Lord and I miss my Albert, I am not ready to see either of them just yet. Tears of joy rolled from my eyes as the doctor left my room.

"I hope you don't mind, I called the Pastor," Maggie said.

I waved my hand to let her know it was okay as I turned my tears away from her. She gently handed me a tissue. I used it to wipe my eyes and gave her a smile. Maggie was a good friend and I knew she wanted the best for me. She stayed for another hour before she had to leave. I sat in my room alone wondering if my actions had alienated everyone. I did not want to die alone.

As I thought of my life and actions I heard a tap on the hospital door.

"Hello, Mother Odell are you awake?" a friendly voice said. To my surprise, it was Pastor Myron and First Lady Deidra. "We heard what happened and rushed to see you. How are you feeling?" She asked.

I was so surprised to have visitors other than Maggie. I told them what the doctor told me and that I would be in recovery for at least a week. They nodded and held my hand, reassuring me that I would be okay. For the first time ever, I thought of them as my Pastor and First Lady. Pastor Myron prayed for me and assured me that I would not have to go through this healing process alone. I was grateful for him and for God sending him.

The Pastor was a man of his word. Everyday First Lady D would stop by my room. She would make sure my flowers were watered. She sat with me and watched television. She even made sure I was being treated fairly by the hospital staff. She was amazing, and I was amazed.

"Could I ask you something?" I said on one of her visits "Why are you being so nice to me. I tried to destroy the vision you had for the church? Yet, you and Pastor have been nothing but kind."

"We battle not against flesh and blood Mother, you know that. My husband and I do not hold anything against you. You were just trying to make sure we did not forget our traditions and who we served. I can assure you we have not. We serve a mighty God one that has healed you. We are grateful for your healing and in serving you we serve God." She said with a beautiful smile.

Chapter 25

Deidra

I slid from under the arm of my husband and headed to the bathroom. Today was another Saturday, which meant another choir practice. The hot mess choir was going to be a little thin today. Several of the members were attending to other obligations. Shonda was still at the hospital most of the day with her son and Mother Odell was also in the hospital. Some of the members called to tell me that they had to work.

I prayed as I showered that the members were not losing hope in the choir. Although they were still a hot mess they were making improvements. I dressed and walked back into the bedroom.

"Good morning, sweetheart off to choir practice?" my husband asked as he rubbed his eyes.

"Hello," I smiled "I am off to choir practice with the hot mess I mean Holy Mass Choir." I corrected myself.

"Thank you." He said with a smile.

I headed to practice, listening to my favorite hymns. I hoped that practice was uneventful today. For the last couple of practices, we have had some sort of issue. As I arrived I counted the cars in the lot. Less than twenty people were present for today's practice.

I was very concerned with how this was going to work. We were supposed to narrow our songs down and select lead parts which is something I am not looking forward to doing. Lead parts meant more arguments. I was not going to do lead parts at all, however, the song called for lead voices. I brainstormed ways around the lead vocal situation before getting out of the car.

The choir had come so far, and I was nervous that singling out a leader would turn it back upside down. I slowly walked into the choir room and found the members talking to each other. This was a change no one was in their own corner or in their clique. I was pleased to see some form of togetherness. They were so wrapped in their conversations and laughter that they did not notice me coming into the choir room.

I smiled.

"Hello everyone, are we ready?"

"Yes!" They said together. I could not help but laugh.

We began practice with an older song that was a favorite among the church members. The voices sounded wonderful. They were all on one accord. Nobody was out of tune or key. I became excited. We practiced three more songs then I got a great idea.

"Guys it is one thing to sing for ourselves and sound wonderful, but it is another thing to sing for others and sound just as wonderful. What would you say to a field trip? We have a couple members in the hospital. I think it would be a blessing to visit them and share this uplifting sound."

To my surprise, the Hot Mess Choir agreed to take our practice on the road. I called one of the deacons so that we could use the church van. Our trip to the hospital was filled with laughter and singing. We enjoyed the thirty- minute ride to the hospital.

Once there we decided to visit Blake first, he was doing better according to his mother and hoped to be going home soon. His accident led to the death of one of his best friends and he was down in his spirit his mother told me. We walked into his room where he sat alone in the dark.

"Hey Blake, I said, "do you mind if I visit with some friends?" I asked.

Blake shrugged his shoulders. I motioned for the choir to come into the room. Blakes face lit up like a Christmas tree when he saw everyone. We promised not to stay long. Blake began to explain that he felt alone and told us that he was grateful that we came to see him. Several of the young guys said that they would visit him once he got home. They joked about playing ball together once Blake was healed completely.

We sang two songs, one of the songs Blake joined in and sang with us. He smiled and ask us if we would save room for him on the choir. He promised that he would recover soon. We assured him that he would always have a spot in the choir and left. He asked us if we would leave the lights on as we walked out the door.

Our next destination was up a few floors of the hospital to Mother Odell's room. I was a little nervous because I was unsure if she would like a group of visitors at once. I had been visiting daily but I was one person. I tapped on her door and asked for permission to enter. I sat with her for a moment and explained the purpose of my visit. She smiled and thanked me for asking for permission to bring a group of people into her room. She adjusted her robe and allowed the choir to enter.

Everyone was nice and gave hugs. They spoke in soft voices and were very respectful.

"So, First Lady tells me you all have a song that is new for me to hear. When are you going to start singing I want to hear it?" Mother Odell said.

We began to sing the song written by our keyboardist. It was a worship song that had an R&B feel to it. Mother listened with a blank expression on her face. She nodded her head slowly as we sang the worship song.

"Young man, you wrote that?" She asked.

"Yes, Mother Odell I wrote it some time ago. What do you think?"

"I think that the Lord has used you to do a mighty work son. You have been blessed with great talent now all you need to do is truly live for Him." She said with a smile.

I let out a sigh of relief because you never know exactly what Mother Odell is going to say. We stayed for a couple minutes singing with Mother Odell. She smiled and laughed with us.

After seeing our sick members, we boarded the church van and headed back to the church. I was excited to tell Myron all the things that happen today. My Hot Mess Choir was coming together.

Chapter 26

Shonda

No matter how disappointed you get in your child you never want to see them hurting. It killed me to see my baby in a hospital bed with tubes cascading out of his broken body. I am so grateful to God that he is getting better and will be home soon.

I attended the funeral service for the young man that died in the car crash. It was a sad event, his mother cried all over the casket. Apparently, he was the driver. Although, the man that hit them had an elevated blood alcohol level and was obviously drunk the report said that the young man was also speeding at the time. This young man also was at fault and because of his stupid choice, he lost his life. He also could have killed two other classmates. My son was wearing his seatbelt, thank God. Although Blake was hurt badly it could have been much worse according to the doctors.

His battle with healing now went past the physical. Mentally he struggled. He felt bad that his friend had died and that another friend would never walk again. Blake had declined visitors from his school. He said he did not want to be bothered. I was pleased to hear that he let the choir come in his room. I was home making sure things were perfect for Blake's arrival. The boys made welcome home signs and we cooked his favorite meal for dinner.

When I walked into his hospital room he was sitting up and getting dressed. I was pleased to see him moving on his own. I shuddered at the thought of losing him. Blake might not be the best kid, but he is my kid.

"You ready to go?" I asked with a smile.

"Yeah, the doctor said I am ready, but I need to wait for a chair. Here is my paperwork," he said handing me a packet of papers detailing his recovery.

We waited for the nurse to bring the wheelchair and packed his get-well cards. He had received cards, balloons, and flowers from classmates. The wife of the drunk driver sent over a card and flowers. She was very remorseful for her husband's actions. She offered to pay for Blake's medical expenses. We were grateful for her willingness to take responsibility for the car accident. She said that she had begged her husband to get help but he refused. She cried with me as I waited for Blake to go into recovery. Although that was a couple of days ago it felt like an eternity.

Once the nurse returned with the wheelchair we headed home. As Blake got into the car it was easy to see that he was still very sore. He gritted his teeth as he sat down in the car. I did my best to drive with care as we went home. We pulled up to the house to see all of the boys outside with signs saying welcome home.

The boys were excited to see Blake and they cheered as he got out of the car. Blake walked in the house and plopped on the couch. I brought out blankets and pillows for him. I figured that the couch would be where he healed. It was at the center of everything. I did not want him to be alone in his room. Although he shared the room he would still be in there by himself for most of the day. I noticed that he would seem sad from time to time. I wanted to make sure that he was surrounded by love.

As the days passed Blake got stronger. He spent more time playing with his brothers. They played video games and he referred their wrestling matches. He was finally acting like the big brother I needed him to be. When one of the boys got out of line he was the first to step in and correct them.

He would allow some friends from school to come by the house and visit while he recovered. I noticed that the friends he had over were not the ones he was hanging with before the accident. He also allowed friends from church to come by the house to visit. This was new for me because I would normally be fussing about his friend choice. God had done something to my son with that accident. He was not the same hard-headed Blake that drove me crazy. This child was different. He helped around the house as much as his body would allow him. He worked in harmony with his brothers and he had a good peer group of friends.

I did not think that there would ever come a day that I would thank God for a horrible experience. Now, I praise God that he brought Blake through it and made him better. I watched Blake interact with his friends and brothers from the kitchen.

We decided to celebrate Blake's recovery with a small get together. Blake had invited a mixture of school friend and church friends. I was so proud of his choices. The kids were all enjoying themselves when Blake came to join me in the kitchen.

"Mom I wanted to tell you that I am sorry. I haven't been the best son. I haven't been the son that you needed me to be and I am sorry. I promise that I will be better and help more. The legal way." He laughed "I promise better choices from now on." He finished and kissed me on the cheek before rejoining his peers and brothers in the living room.

Chapter 27

Donnell

I was sleep when my phone rang. I had a hard time finding the phone that was lost in my blankets.

"Hello. Tiffany. What. I can barely hear you. What! What! Okay, I am on my way. I am on my way!" frantically I dressed and raced out of the house.

I assumed God was on my side because I did not get a ticket as I drove eighty miles an hour to Tiffany's apartment. The apartment was surrounded by police officers and police cars. Red and Blue lights flashed in the darkness. My heart nearly jumped out of my chest as I approached the apartment.

The door to Tiffany's apartment was wide open and looked as if someone tried to take it off the hinges. There was blood covering the door and the walls of the apartment. I saw Tiffany sitting on the torn-up couch talking to the police.

She had been beaten badly. Her face was full of scratches and blood. She had broken all of her nails and her head was missing hair in spots. Tears filled her eyes when she realized I was standing in the room.

"He is okay," she told the police "he is my daughter's father. Eva sweetie daddy is here." She called Eva.

Eva ran to me and jumped into my arms.

"Daddy," she whispered, "he hurt mommy."

"Did he hurt you?" I whispered back.

I was relieved when she shook her head no. My heart sank to the pit of my stomach. I was sad for Tiffany, but I would have been very angry if something would have happened to my baby. I asked the police officer what the plan was going to be, I made it known that I wanted to take Eva with me. The officer said that if Tiffany agreed that would be fine. I looked at Tiffany. My stare said everything I needed to say. Tiffany shook her head, yes and I went to gather Eva's things.

Despite the condition of the house and the swelling of her face Tiffany told the police that she did not want to press charges against her attacker that sat in the police car outside. She swore that it was just a misunderstanding and that she was at just as much fault as he was. With that said I knew that Eva could never return to Tiffany.

Tiffany was so adamant about not pressing charges and being involved that the police decided to take both Tiffany and her newest man to jail. I took Eva's clothes, they all needed to be washed and a couple of toys for her to play with. I tried to shield her eyes from seeing the cops handcuff her mother. I took Eva to the car and fastened her into her car seat. I watch the police take Tiffany to jail.

By the time we arrived at my house, Eva was sleeping in the back seat. I took her out of the car and placed her in my bed. I could no longer sleep.

I took her dirty clothes and put them in the washing machine. Tears filled my eyes. I wondered what the Lord was doing and why had he allowed my baby to witness such violence. I was determined to do everything that I could to keep her from her mother. Eva was the love of my life. Just then my mind shifted to Stacey. I loved her so much and knew that she would make a great mother. I, however, was unsure if she wanted to be Eva's mother.

Eva's conception and birth led to her broken heart. I needed to be sure she was ready for this type of journey. While the clothes washed I opened my laptop. I begin to look up information on getting custody of Eva. I knew it was going to be a hard fight. It was not easy to take a child away from its mother in my state. It seemed the more I researched the more I felt defeated.

There are many laws that support mothers and children. I could find very few laws that supported fathers. I held my head in my hand as the phone rang.

"Donnell, it is me, Tiffany. Look I need you to come to get me. Please. I need you to bail me out."

"What! Man, you done lost your mind. No!"

"What do you mean no, you have my daughter. Come get me!"

"No man, and I have my daughter. If I have my way, bump that I am going to have my way and you will not be keeping my daughter."

"What!"

"You heard me, I'm keeping Eva!" I said.

"You can't do that. No one is going to give that baby girl to you." She laughed.

"Laugh all you want from jail Tiffany, you ain't never getting Eva back and that's real."

"Whatever Donnell, you going to come and get me?"

"No!" I said and hung up the phone.

How dare she call me and ask me to pick her up from jail after what she put Eva through. She must truly be out of her mind. I went to put Eva's clothes in the dryer and realized they needed to be washed again. As I put the clothes back into the washer I became more determined to get custody of my child.

I went to my bedroom and stood by the door. Eva was curled up in my bed sleeping like an angel. Her little body looked like a pillow in my massive bed. I returned to my research after checking on Eva.

I found cases where fathers gained custody of their kids after some fighting. I found a lawyer that specializes in supporting single dads. I thought it was cool that someone was out there on the side of fathers. So much of the information I found was about fathers not doing what they needed to do as men. That may be the case for some but not for all and not for me. I placed Eva's clothes in the dryer, after two washes they came clean.

That is when I knew this was going to be an uphill battle.

Chapter 28

Mother Odell

It is not until you are in the hospital alone do you realize how alone you are. I stared at the open door to my room. No one came to see me except for the Pastor and First Lady. Maggie visited when she could but that was not often. Had it not been for those three people I would be totally alone.

I grew tired of watching television. Maggie had brought my Bible from my house I promise I felt like I had read halfway through the Bible by the time they started talking about discharging me. I was concerned about going home because I was all alone.

My heart grew heavy. I was unsure of what I was going to do about being home alone. I had no family in the area. My closest relative lived an hour away in the next town. She claimed that she did not have transportation and could not come see me while I was in the hospital. I knew that staying with her would be out of the question.

"Ms. Odell, do you have any questions about aftercare. You should be going home in a few days?" Doctor Johnson asked.

Dr. Johnson was a tall thin main. He had long muscles that blanketed his body. His goatee was manicured and so were his nails. I thought he would be a great catch for one of the single sisters at church.

"What all will I need to do when I get a home doctor?"

"Well, I suggest you lose some weight and monitor your blood pressure. You should also try to exercise at least three times a week."

"That sounds easy enough."

"And you need to make sure you take your medicine regularly."

"Okay, can I ask you something doctor?"

"Sure."

"Do you believe in the Lord?"

"I sure do that is why I became a doctor. To be a part of the healing process."

"Do you have a church home?"

"Yes, I do. My wife and I attend Grace Love."

Darn, I thought I had found a husband for one of those sisters at church. I let the doctor go back to his rounds and sat bored. I hated being in the hospital. There was nothing for me to get into, nothing for me to do but sit. I thought about my actions toward Deidra and the choir. I was a little embarrassed by my behavior. Even though I was completely out of place she never once disrespected me. She always maintained her Proverbs 31 stance. If it was not for her I would only have one visitor.

Deidra came to see me at least four times a week. I was surprised that she treated me with such kindness and love. She was a special girl. I was glad that she was the First Lady of the church. She still needed to stop wearing those pants but other than that she was okay with me.

"Mother Odell, how are you today?" Deidra said as she walked into my hospital room. She wore a nice floral dress. I smiled she looked like a pastor's wife.

"I am doing fine dear, come on in."

"What have you been doing, watching television?"

"No, I was trying to get that fine doctor to come to church. But he is married so it would not do the single ladies at church no good if he came."

"Mother! You can't be in the hospital hooking people up that ain't Godly. Besides you are supposed to be in here healing."

"Well, some of the sisters at the church need a little healing. A little Marvin Gaye type of healing."

"Mother! Oh my God. I can believe you said that! I am going to have to check your medicine list. What these people been given you that has got you so fresh."

"Child I am an old woman and when you get my age you say what you want to say. When you survive a heart attack you do what you want and thank God that you can live to do it."

She smiled and nodded. She was really a sweet girl when I took the time to get to know her. She changed my flowers and dusted the windows for me. She sat, and we talked about church.

I told her that I really enjoyed when the choir came by to sing. I even like the song that the keyboard player wrote more than I thought I would. I had to be honest, however, I still was not sold on the keyboard player. There was something about him that made me want to ask questions. Deidra assured me that it was all in my head and that I was just being messy.

I laughed and did not take offense to being called messy. I suppose I was a little messy. Like I told Deidra when you get my age you can do that. I am well aware that I do messy well. But hey it is me.

Deidra stayed for another hour and we watched television together. We laughed at the couple on television trying to solve their problems without the help of the Lord. We talked about the absence of Christian entertainment. She told me that she had some Urban Christian Fiction books that I should read and about some Christian films that were coming out. I told her that I would love to read the books she recommended.

Deidra had become like a daughter to me. Her visits made us closer and I got to know her for the woman of God that she was. I hoped that once I was out of the hospital she would still come and see me. I felt better after our visit and looked forward to spending time together outside of the hospital.

Chapter 29

Deidra

I woke up before the alarm clock went off. In fact, I was dressed and ready to go to choir practice before the clock sounded. Today I was going to assign lead parts for the songs I thought we might sing. It was still up to the choir to select the songs we would sing but I wanted to be prepared.

I dressed in pants because I did not know what the day would bring. I prayed that we grew past a time of fighting and arguing but I could not be sure. Things change when you start assigning special duties to people. The choir could decide they did not like my selections and start drama. I prayed that everyone would celebrate the chosen.

As I drove to church I thought about the people I selected for lead parts in the songs. I had prayed about my decision and was at peace with the leaders. Pulling up to the church I noticed Shonda had brought all the boys including Blake. I was glad that Blake was feeling better and was able to attend practice. I walked in the packed choir room and began to take roll. I noticed that Donnell was not in attendance. I looked toward Stacey and she shrugged her shoulders. She seemed to be just as surprised as I was that he was not in choir practice.

"Today guys is a big day. We will try out some of you as lead voices for some of the songs that we sing." I said.

The choir cheered. I thought that was a good sign as to how this would go. For the first song, I selected Stacey as lead singer. Stacey had a powerful voice and that was exactly what the song called for a strong voice.

Stacey smiled as she walked to the front of the room and grabbed the microphone. I queued the music and then the choir. Stacey's voice was perfect for the song. We sounded wonderful. We sang so good that some of the members began to cry as they sung.

The second song was to be led by Shonda's twin boys. I asked her if it was okay for them to sing lead. She was pleased and said yes. The boys were so excited to sing in front of everyone. Although some of the members were surprised at my choice they did not complain about having kids lead the song.

At the age of fourteen, the boys' voices had not completely changed. They still had smooth tenor voices. They sang the first verse of the song and then the choir joined in the song. They sounded like professional singers. The sound that came from their voices went straight to heaven.

The third song was my husband's favorite song. He would often play it when he needed encouragement. I wanted this song to be special because he loved it so much. I decided that I would surprise him and sing the lead for the song. The choir was shocked that I was able to lead the song. They had never heard me sing before.

We practiced each song at least three times. Each time we sounded better. I was very pleased with the outcome of practice.

"First Lady I know that we are supposed to pick the three songs out of the six that we know, but can we just sing these three with the leads. They sound so good and I am blessed by them. I know that others will be blessed too." One of the members said.

I looked at the choir to see what they thought. Most of them nodded in agreement. I was pleased that we were coming together. We took a voted and everyone agreed that we would sing the three songs with the lead singers. We practiced one more round of the songs.

I remembered that my husband offered to buy the choir lunch one practice. I called Myron to confirm that buying lunch was still okay. He was on board and excited that I was thinking about taking the choir on an outing.

The choir was excited about going to the all you can eat restaurant for lunch once I explained that it was my treat. I called the deacon and had him bring two of the church vans so that we could be comfortable.

"Lady D, I really appreciate you buying lunch, but I am going to have to skip out. I have not heard from

Donnell and I want to go and see if he is okay." Stacey said with a concerned look on her face.

"Sure, sweetie I understand. Let him know if he needs anything we are here for him." I said.

As the choir got in the vans I could not help but thank God. He had brought the choir to another level. I listened in on the conversations that the members were having as we drove to the restaurant. They were being nice to each other. They talked amongst themselves regardless of the choir that they came from. Young members and older members spoke to each other. They laughed and joked together. My heart was overjoyed. I finally understood what my husband was trying to do with the choir. He had unified them.

We ate together as one choir family. The children sat with some of the older members and they playfully compared plate sizes. The young adults and the adults had interesting conversations about ways to serve the Lord. I had several conversations with members about ways to take our choir unity to the church.

Some of the members asked me about my singing. They did not know that I had such a beautiful voice. I told them about my background in music and my years performing with choirs and music groups.

"Well, why didn't you tell us that in the beginning?" One of the members said.

I laughed and explained that I did not want to come in sounding uppity. Shonda laughed and said that I was one of the humblest women of God she knew.

Chapter 30

Shonda

I was grateful that we were invited to lunch. Nobody can imagine what it is like feeding six growing boys. The boys had a great time full of smiles and laughter. They ate several plates and I hoped that meant I did not need to prepare dinner.

On the van ride back, Blake sat with some of the teenagers from the choir. I overheard them talking about forming a teen choir for the community. I smiled because God was answering my prayer and my son was changing. We arrived at the church and waddled to my car. As we got near the car a group of boys approached Blake, who was walking in front of me and the other boys.

"Man, what's up we ain't seen you around?" One of the boys said to Blake.

"Ain't nothing just ain't on that no more that's all. Besides I got my brothers to look after."

"Shoot I keep my brother with me. That don't change anything. You should come hang out with us bring you, little brothers, too."

"Naw, man I ain't on that. I told you. I'm living differently." Blake said, and we got into the car as a family and drove home.

Once home I expected Blake to want to hang out late as always. But he did not even ask. He played video games with the twins instead. I did not want to get my hopes up, but it seemed like things were getting better. I asked him to go to the store for me and he did not put up a fight. He said that he would be taking Byron and Bradley with him. That was fine with me because I knew he was trying to spend time with all the boys.

I decided that while I waited for the boys to return I would do some laundry. I put a load in the washer and grabbed a book. I love sitting in my laundry room. It is the one place where I know the boys won't come in and hold conversations with me. They are afraid that I might ask them to help. I sat and enjoyed the sound of the washer as I read. Once the clothes are washed I put them in the dryer and start another load. I noticed the time and realized that Blake and the boys had not returned from the store. I thought, maybe I should have let Blake drive, but the store was only a mile from my house.

I did another load of laundry before I began to worry. Something was not right with this situation. The boys had been gone for over an hour. I brought the laundry into the living room. As I placed it on the floor Bryon raced in the house calling my name. I ran outside to see Blake slumped over and bloody.

"Oh my God, oh my God!" I said as I raced to Blake's side.

I looked around to see if any of the other boys were hurt. I thanked God that they were okay. I grabbed Blake and led him into the house and on the couch.

"What in God's name happened?" I asked as I motioned for one of the boys to bring Blake a water bottle that was sitting on the kitchen counter.

Blake just came home from the hospital and I was scared that he was going to have to go back. He had two black eyes and blood on his knuckles. His jaw looked like it was swollen, and his lip was burst. My baby had been beaten badly.

"Mama, it was these boys, right. I think they were the ones from church today. So, they come up to us right and start talking junk about how you can't just stop hanging out and stuff. How you one of them or you not. Then the big one was like so what's it gonna be? You down or not? And Blake looked at us and he put us behind him and said naw man I can't. That when it was like BAM they started beating him up. We tried to jump in but Blake would not let us. He kept pushing us back every free chance he got. He had one of them, dudes, he beat him up pretty good but when they all jumped in, well you see him." Bradley said.

Tears filled my eyes, but I knew this was no time to cry. I walked Blake to the bathroom to help him get cleaned up. He did not say a word until we got to the bathroom.

"I am sorry mama." He said with tears in his eyes.

"Shhh."

"No, I need to say this, I am sorry mama. I am sorry for making you worry. I am sorry for living opposite of how you were trying to raise me. I am sorry that I could have got my brothers hurt today. I am sorry. Those boys I use to run with, but as I told them I am not on that no more. Unfortunately, it ain't that easy to let them go. But it is over now. I am through with it and them. I just pray that the other boys don't get caught up in that stuff as I did."

I began to cry as I listen to him confess his wrongdoing.

"Don't cry, mama. It was not your fault. I was hard-headed and thought I knew everything." He said as he wiped the blood from his face.

I held my son and cried anyway. He was alive, and he could have been dead. He seemed to be turning over a new leaf and I was grateful to God.

"Should we call the police? We should call the police." I said.

"No mama, we should not. I said it is okay and it is trust me." He said trying to smile for my sake.

Chapter 31

Donnell

Thank God I had a lot of paid time off stored up. I was able to take the entire week off to be with Eva. I could have sent her to preschool but from what I was told on the phone she had not been attending regularly. Her mother had kept her home so much that they had given her spot away. Although, they were willing to work with me given my current situation I decided to just stay home with Eva.

I was surprised the Eva slept as much as she did in my bed. She would often wake up by lunchtime even if I put her to bed early. I assumed that she did not get much sleep in her mother's house. I also suspected that she was more comfortable, sleeping on clean sheets in a clean room. At her mother's house things were unkept and often she would have parties late at night. My poor baby probably never got much sleep while living with her mother.

If I had anything to do with it, she would not have to worry about living with her mother. I was already in contact with a lawyer. He said that I had a chance although it was going to be a battle. I would fight as long and as hard as I needed to fight. God as my witness, Eva was not going to live with Tiffany again.

I kicked myself for ever getting involved with Tiffany. But the devil knew how to tempt me. She was a beautiful woman. She had curves in all the right places. Her hair, nails, and makeup were on point. She smelt like a gift. I was taken away at first sight. Little did I know she was crazy and manipulative. If it had not been for the DNA test I would not have believed that Eva was my child. I thought she was lying the whole pregnancy. I was in love with Stacey and thought Tiffany was just trying to get back at me because I did not want a relationship with her.

When the results came back, and I found out that Eva was mine, I rushed to her side. I held Eva for the first time and fell deeply in love with her. Eva was and always has been my main priority. God blessed me with her to keep me straight. Prior to Eva, I was a little reckless. I loved the Lord, but I was still reckless in my actions. Eva entered my life and all of that changed. I became a better man and a better Christian. I wanted to be the best I could be for Eva and that meant being the best I could be for God.

As Eva slept I did some work on the computer. I looked up statues and cases similar to mine. I wanted to be prepared for the fight I was getting ready to enter. I missed choir practice, but I was not concerned with that at the time. My heart said that I should have called Stacey, but I was so busy. I had been meaning to update her all week but that did not happen. I never knew how much energy you needed to take care of a three- year- old. I was looking in the cabinet to figure out lunch when I heard a knock at my front door. I was not expecting visitors, so I walked slowly to the door.

"Well hello, stranger," Stacey said.

"Hey, babe come in," I said opening the door. I hugged her as she walked into the house.

"You have been missing, no phone calls and you missed practice that is not like you. What is up?"

"Things have been complicated. How was practice?"

"Great, I am singing lead on one of the songs."

"Wow, babe that is great!"

"So, you gonna tell me what you have been doing?"

"Like I said it has been complicated babe, Tiffany got arrested and now I have Eva. I took the week off work, so I could handle some things for Eva. Her situation with her mom is very messed up. I don't know how but I can't let her go back to her mother. I have been doing some research and I think I found a lawyer. He said I had a chance."

"So, you are going to be a full-time dad?"

"I have always been a full- time dad there is nothing I will not do for my child. I am just working on her being here with me full- time."

"I see."

"Why do you look concerned?"

"I was just wondering where I fit into your plan?"

"What do you mean, you fit where you have always fit. I love you Stacey. That has not changed. I promise never to hurt you, that has not changed. I just have this on my plate now, that is all."

"Okay. Well, where is she?"

"Sleep. Believe it or not she sleeps a lot. I don't think she got a lot of sleep at her mother's house."

"Aw poor thing. I am sure she is excited to be here. You seem to have everything she needs." Stacey said as she looked around and saw the toys I brought Eva.

Stacey seemed a little nervous. She sat straight up in her seat on the couch. She had tension in her face and she did not seem as relaxed as she would normally be in my home. We watched a movie until Eva woke up. Then I fixed us all lunch. I suggested that we go to the park, but Stacey said she was fine sitting here watching movies. We watched a couple of family-friendly movies before Stacey said she had other errands to run. I kissed her on the cheek and watched her walk out of the door. Something in my heart began to hurt, she was my true love, but the love of my life was sitting on my couch watching cartoons.

Chapter 32

Mother Odell

I praised God as I got dressed. I finally felt well enough to go to a Sunday service. I missed church and was looking forward to being a part of the worship. I had something to shout about. God had healed my body and delivered my mind. I was determined to go and show the Lord how much I appreciated the blessings. I went to the kitchen to fix my breakfast. I had oatmeal and fresh fruit. I put on my new Sunday dress. I had lost some weight and needed a new dress for this Sunday. Maggie was nice enough to take me to pick up something. I was able to get a few new things to go with my new body. I still had a great deal of weight to lose but I was on the right track.

After I dressed and ate I headed to church. I was pleased that I was able to find a parking spot close to the front of the church. I walked in everyone was pleased to see me. The ushers greeted me with a smile several of them were members of the Hot Mess Choir with me. I chuckled at the thought of the Hot Mess Choir. I wondered what my First Lady would think if she knew that I called her choir the Hot Mess Choir instead of the Holy Mass Choir. She would probably say that I was being messy, and I would have to agree with her.

I took my seat in the Mother's section on the second row. The Senior Choir was scheduled to sing today's selections. Normally I would sing with them, but I had been sick. I noticed that although it was Senior Choir Sunday the church was filled with both young and old people. This was something new. In the past Senior Choir Sunday meant that the young people and the adults would skip out on church. This Sunday everyone was present to worship and praise together. I was pleased to see everyone was present.

The choir sang, and worship erupted in the building. People were shouting at the glory of the Lord. The ushers were busy handing out fans and tissues. Several of the sisters became slain in the spirit and the ushers covered them with purple sheets. The atmosphere was high, the spirit of the Lord was moving in the building. I could feel the warmth and comfort of the Lord. I was grateful to be back.

The First Lady came over to me during the part of service where we greeted one another.

"Mother Odell, it is so good to see you out today. I am so glad you were able to join us, and you look great." She said.

"Thank you, baby, I feel great. God is good."

"All the time."

"And all the time,"

"God is good." We said together.

We sat back down in our respective seats as the Pastor came up to speak. He wore his pastoral robe which usually meant that the word was going to be extra special that day. He was a great big man and he towered over the pulpit. He cleared his throat before speaking.

"Church today we are going to talk about the greatest of all the commandments. Today we are going to speak on love. Now we may like to believe that we can choose who we love but that is not the case. The Bible is very specific on who we should love. We should love everybody!" He began.

As he preached his sermon I began to think about how he and his wife treated me. How despite what I did or said they showed me respect and love. They could have cussed me out and told me where to go and how fast to get there. However, they did not do that. They loved me. They spoke respectfully to me, they listened to me and they did not come at me even after I went after them. I chuckled as I recalled telling the church they were all going to Hell. Even with me saying that the Pastor still showed me, love. He could have had me sat down as a mother, but he did not. He just loved me. In fact, being honest he and his wife loved the hell out of me.

They came to visit me in the hospital and to pray. Sweet First Lady Deidra came to my room at least four times a week to see about me. She did more for me then my niece who only lives an hour away. She even came to the house after I was home to see about me. She brought me food and the church bulletin. We would talk about anything I wanted to talk about, she was so sweet. After I had been nothing but evil to her she was still sweet as pie. As the Pastor spoke about love I could not help but examine his walk. He wasn't just up there telling people what they should do. He was telling them how he was able to do it. The Pastor was a man of God's word. Although I missed some of the traditional parts of church I had to admit I loved the fact that the Pastor lived what he preached. I was refreshed by his leadership.

After the Word was brought forth the choir sang another song. They sang one of my favorite hymns.

"Mother Odell, if you don't mind and you are up to it will you sing with us. We are so glad to have you back" the choir director said.

The churched cheered and encouraged me to sing with the choir. I was taken back by the love and unity they showed me. I was the same woman that condemned them to Hell, yet they showed me, love. I gladly joined the choir and sang my favorite old hymn with them.

Chapter 33

Deidra

"Hey beautiful, where are you off to?" Myron asked as he woke up.

"It is Saturday babe, Holy Mass Choir practice. You know that. I don't want to be late." I said as I put on my shoes. I wasn't late, in fact, I was a little early.

"Well okay. Have a nice practice." He added as I headed out of the door.

I doubled back to his bedside to kiss him before I left, then I raced out of the door. On the drive to practice, I hummed the song I was leading in the choir. Once there I was pleased to see that the parking lot was full. A full parking lot meant that everyone would be in the building and ready to practice on time. I even noticed that Mother Odell's car was in the parking lot. I was glad that she was able to join us again.

When I walked in the choir room all the members were talking amongst themselves. They were not in any particular order nor were they with their main choir group. I started the practice with roll call. This time everybody joined in and sang the word we are here. Mother Odell was the first to sing for the Senior Choir she held the last note of here and added some vocal runs at the end. The choir erupted in praise.

The first song we practiced required everyone to rock from side to side. Normally this would have been a disaster with members bumping into one another. However, this time they were able to move together as one group. The children were in step, the young adults and adults were not running into each other. All I could do was smile.

We practiced the next selection which had Stacey's solo in the middle of the song. The song was about not leaning on your own understanding and letting the Lord guide you. I am not sure what Stacey had going on, but she sang that song with all of her might. As she sang I could see the tears forming in Donnell's eyes. She sang like she meant every word that she said.

After Stacey's song, we took a break so that the children could use the restroom. I noticed again how united the choir was. Several members went to comfort Stacey who was in tears. Once the break was over everyone went right back to their places so that we could start the next song.

I was shocked there was no complaining. There was not one bitter word about the song choice. Everyone was on one accord and singing unto the glory of the Lord.

Tears filled my eyes as the choir sang the next song. I could not contain my joy. I found myself shouting and praising the name of the Lord. Several of the members joined me in praise. We sang of God's love, how He never changes and how He is always there when we need Him. I thought about how that love was shown through the choir. I thought about how God had taken a Hot Mess Choir and turned it into a Holy Mass Choir. He had changed the hearts of the members in the choir. He had also changed the hearts of the members of the church. Church members now greeted each other in love. They showed greater respect toward one another and they looked out for one another. I could not help but praise after all that God had done for Holy Missionary Baptist Church.

After the practice, everyone gathered around for final announcements. We started by thanking God for the practice and for healing our members. We prayed for Brother Donnell and his daughter.

"Choir I can't begin to describe how proud I am to be your director," I said. "You all have come such a long way. I know that God is looking down on us and saying well done. I must be honest I use to refer to us as the Hot Mess Choir because we were a hot mess. Truth is though all of us are still a hot mess." They choir broke out in laughter. "Let me tell you why I say that," I began again. "we all have mess in our lives, things that we are going through. The enemy is always on his job trying to keep us from our purpose. Life can get, does get and is at times a hot mess. But choir we can't did not and don't let that stop our praise. We must praise when life is going great and we must praise when life is a hot mess. We cannot allow our praise to be taken away. Our praise is our weapon against the troubles of this world. It is our defense against the messiness that we face. That is why it was so important that we come together as one. So that we can send all the angels to flight on the church's behalf. We are a mess and may even be a hot mess at times, but God still blessed amen." I said, and the choir said amen after me.

With those words, we were dismissed, and everyone prepared themselves to go about their day. Some left singing others chatting with new friends. I sat for a moment before going home to tell Myron about today's practice.

"Oh, Myron you should have been there," I said "everyone was on one accord and everyone was singing and praising together. There was no fighting or complaining it was wonderful. We were not a hot mess we were something that God blessed, and He is going to use us, Myron! I know He is!" I said to Myron as I rushed in the door. I could not contain myself. Myron smiled and nodded as he hugged and kissed me.

Chapter 34

Shonda

I decided that since the boys were doing so well I would take them to a theme park. We don't get out often but when I can save up I try to take them somewhere. It took a lot of overtime and long hours, but I was able to save enough to take them to the small theme park in our city. It had been years since they all were able to go. I thanked God for overtime and packed a lunch.

When we arrived at the park the boys wanted to all do different things. I was able to split them into groups and allow them to run free in the park. Luckily for them, the park was enclosed so there was no worry about them being taken. They were at the age where kidnapping was the least of my worries. I worried more about them on the street than at a theme park.

All of the boys went their separate ways except for Blake, he decided to walk with me. I was grateful for the company. He had grown so much over the last couple of months. Sure, he was the same height and weight, but he was a more mature young man. His decisions were different. He was more responsible and helpful.

I enjoyed walking with him. We talked about his brothers. He said he never wanted them to learn or go through what he went through over the past few months. He explained that he learned the hard way and he would not wish that on anyone. He was very serious about his life being different.

"Well son, you are growing up soon you will be out for real. What schools have you thought about attending for college?" I asked hoping that he had thought about his future.

He smiled and continued to walk with me. He grabbed my hand as we walked. I wondered what he was going to say. He had not held my hand since he was a small child. His actions made me a little nervous. I thought he was going to say something crazy.

"Well, I have actually thought about it a lot. It is going to sound crazy."

"Why?"

"Because I have never told anyone, not yet anyway."

"So, what is it?"

"I don't know how to say it out loud. I mean I am young, but I know I am not going to change my mind."

"Okay."

"I just do not know if people will believe me."

"Son, it does not matter what people think. If you are sure then that is what matters."

"Humm"

"I am serious, what you want to do and be is between you and God. I will support whatever it is. I trust you. But more importantly, I trust the God in you. I have watched God do a mighty work in you and I know that whatever it is you would like to do will be successful. All you need to do is believe in yourself. Don't be scared."

"I hear you mom, thank you."

"Don't thank me, tell me. What is it that you are thinking about doing."

"Oh, I am not thinking, I know for sure what I am supposed to do."

"Okay well, can I know?"

He laughed and kissed my hand. I thought for a minute Lord this boy is going to say something crazy and I am going to have to repent for cussing.

"Well mama, I feel that I have been called to preach and minister to young men." He said looking me in the eye.

I stood speechless and puzzled for a moment. I was unsure of what my next action should be. My heart wanted to leap. My soul wanted to run. My mouth wanted to shout. But in the end, my eyes won as they decided to cry.

"Mama why are you crying?" he asked

"Because I am happy son. From the bottom of my soul, I am happy. You cannot imagine how happy I am."

We continued to walk through the park holding hands. I thought back to the nights I stayed up praying and worrying where my son might be. I thought about all the tears I shed over him. I thought about the phone calls from jail and from the hospital. I could not help thinking about all the people that mocked me. The ones that laughed at the fact that I had six kids and five baby daddies. I thought about how they counted me and my kids out. I thought about how they assumed that Blake and the other boys would all be dead or in jail.

Then I thought about God and how he said he would give me the desires of my heart. I thought about how God not man honors your faithfulness. I smiled as I held my son's hand as we walked in the theme park.

"Mom do you know what my steps should be to become a preacher? I suppose I should speak with Pastor Myron." He asked puzzled and excited.

"I think that will be a great idea. I am sure he can recommend a college for you to attend and give you some small experience in leadership at the church."

"That would be great. I want to start a mentoring program for young men to keep them off the street. I think that the church and the community could benefit from the program. It would not be big at first, but I can see it growing into something great for everyone."

"Son I think that is an amazing idea and I am sure Pastor Myron and the church leadership will love that idea as well. We are all so proud of the man you are becoming." I said.

We finished our walk and met up with the other boys for lunch. I left that park feeling blessed and praising God for deliverance.

Chapter 35

Donnell

I sat dressed in my Sunday suit on the courthouse bench. Eva sat on my lap dressed in a lavender dress that I bought for her the day before we needed to be in court. Tiffany showed up with her latest boyfriend dressed in her best club dress. I could not stand to look at her. My lawyer spoke first then Tiffany who decided to represent herself had words for the judge.

It did not take the judge long to come back with a verdict. He was very clear on the instructions he had for Tiffany. I was granted temporary custody of Eva. My lawyer explained that this was the first step. He assured me that I would have Eva full-time.

I left the courtroom with Eva and a big smile. Tiffany did not bother to say goodbye to Eva nor did she seem to care that I had won. She waved us off and put her arms around her new man. As we walked down the stairs of the court house I called Stacey.

She was so excited she screamed on the phone. I told her that it was not over yet. I explained that I still had a battle ahead of me and that my custody was only temporary. She said that it was still great news and that she could not wait to see us.

I loved the sound of that "us". I drove home and put Eva down for a nap. There were so many things that I needed to do. I had used all of my sick and vacation time and needed to find a school for Eva. I also needed to find a bigger apartment. We would not last long in my one bedroom. Eva was accumulating too many toys and clothes. My huge closet was running out of the room. All I could think about was getting things prepared for my little girl. Then I thought about Stacey. I had been so busy with Eva that I had not spent much time with her. I was focused on getting my daughter situated.

Stacey was so kind that she did not fuss me out for forgetting to call or breaking our dates because Eva needed me. I loved her. I thought about my promise to her. I had sworn never to hurt her again. I remember how she cried when she found out about Eva. She was heartbroken. She cried in my chest and I cried as well. We were meant to be then, but God had a plan bigger than either of us. His plan was that beautiful baby girl sleeping in my bed.

Stacey and I would have to take a break until now. Now we were close friends and we had firm understanding that it was God who had the final say in our lives. We both trusted and believed in His plan. To us, God's plan was what was most important regardless of how we felt. I took a deep breath and called Stacey. Her sweet voice on the other end of the phone made me smile. God knows how much I loved that girl. She agreed to come over and said she was looking forward to spending time with Eva and me. I smiled, as tears entered my eyes I hung up the phone.

Stacey came over just as Eva was waking up from her nap. I answered the door with Eva in my arms. Stacey smiled and offered to hold Eva as soon as she saw her.

"My, she has got so big in such a short time," Stacey said.

"Yes. Hey, put her over there with her toys so we can talk." I said.

Stacey put her down and I grabbed her hand and led her to my couch. She was so beautiful that it hurt me to think of what I needed to tell her.

"Baby, I love you. I love you so much. You have been truly my God sent. I promised that I would never hurt you again and I meant that. Never again would make you doubt or cry. My lawyer says that I have a battle on my hands, but he thinks I can win. I just need to make sure everything is in place. That means a lot of things, I have to move, find child care and work out something with my job. There is a lot for me to do. I don't want you to think that I am neglecting you. You deserve someone that is going to be there for you. Right now, I cannot promise that can be me. Instead of us breaking up and hating each other I think it is best we stay friends." Tears rolled down my cheek. I hated every word I said but I knew it was for the best.

I needed to be there for my daughter. She had to be my focus. Stacey looked at me with tears in her eyes. She wiped my face with her hand. She kissed me softly on my lips. She stared at me quietly for a moment as if she was trying to process all that I had said.

"Donnell, I love you. I love Eva. I understand that you have a battle on your hands and that you will not have time like you did when you were completely single. I understand all that trust me. But I love you too much to walk away. I love you too much to let you go through this battle alone. I love Eva too much not to be in her life. So, if you will allow me I would like to fight with you and grow this relationship with you." She said.

I kissed her long and hard. We agreed to take it slowly. She understood that Eva was top priority but that was not going to stop our love for one another. We held each other and watched Eva play with her toys on the floor in front of us.

Chapter 36

Mother Odell

The Lord sure is funny sometimes He knows how to get you. I sat in church on Bible Study night listening to Pastor Myron. He was teaching on gifts in preparation for his sermon on unity for the Pastor's Anniversary Celebration.

He explained to the church that God can use all of our gifts. He said that God gave us gifts to enhance the kingdom of God. I chuckled to myself as I thought of my gifts. God sure was funny. I had a talent for wanting order and speaking up when something was not right. According to my Pastor, the kingdom needed my gifts. He said without them the saints might get too worldly and cut the fool.

"Not on my watch Pastor!" I shouted

"Amen." He laughed as he finished his word.

Toward the end of the service, he asked if anyone wanted to come up and testify to the things God called them to be. Just like that Bible study turned into testimony service. A line of members began to form.

Members were testifying how God called them to be better fathers and mothers. They said how God called them to take the word of God into the community. The one that took my heart was Shonda's son, the bad one. He got up there dressed like a decent young man.

"Giving honor to God who is the head of my life. To the Pastor and leadership. My name is Blake. God has given me a gift. He has called me to preach his word to young people and to help them get out of trouble." He said as his mama shouted in the background.

I said amen because God often uses the bad ones. I knew that one of them boys of hers was going to do something positive. Heck, she had so many all of them could not be rotten apples. I smiled as the young man hugged the Pastor and some of the leaders. I was happy for his mama she had worked so hard for those boys.

I felt a tug in my spirit and decided that I should join the line. I walked up to the line and overheard some of the saints whispering.

"Oh Lord, what is she doing."

"She is finna give it to us."

"You know she is a trip"

I heard every word, but I did not let that stop me from getting in the line to testify. I waited patiently behind all those with gifts that nervously told the church what God had called them to be and do.

When it was my turn I grabbed the microphone and stared out into the church.

"Yes, I know that I can be a trip. As my spiritual daughter, Lady Deidra says I can be messy sometimes. Yes, I know. I also know when God wants me to speak. He always prompts me to speak the truth. The truth church is that I do not have a Heaven or Hell to put you in. The truth is I was wrong. But I have learned that hurt people, hurt people. I was hurting but our First Lady did not let the fact that I was hurting her change how she dealt with me. She still treated me with love and respect. She came to see about me when my own family would not. God used her to heal my brokenness. Watching her walk taught me so much about my own. I learned. I am an old woman, but God sent a young one to teach me, so I know she can teach you. I stand before you today proclaiming that God is good and that he will give you everything you need." I said as tears filled my eyes. Deidra came up and gave me a great big hug and whispered that she loved me. I shouted to the glory of the Lord as I took my seat.

After service, the Pastor and his lovely wife invited me to dinner with them. We went to a small spot that served soul food. I was mindful of my choices although I did have a great meal. We spoke about the direction of the church. The Pastor had a big vision to do things for the community and to take the message of Christ into the city. I was grateful that he chose to share his thoughts with me. He also said that his wife would be doing some teaching and he wanted to know if I would join her in teaching the woman of the church.

"I think the two of you would be wonderful and a blessing to the women of the church." He said as he ate.

"Well, Pastor I don't know what to say?" I said pondering the thought of teaching a class. Teaching is something that Albert, my late husband, always encouraged me to do. Our last pastor felt that he was the only one that should speak to his flock.

"Mother say yes," Deidra said

"Mother say what God would have you say." Pastor Myron corrected his wife.

I smiled.

"Yes, I would love to work with the First Lady and teach the women of the church," I said.

We continued to eat and plan for our classes. The first class we were going to teach was on a deeper intimacy with the Lord. It would focus on hearing from the Lord, studying His word and prayer. I was excited about our new venture together. I knew that God was going to do something grand in my life and in the life of Deidra.

I laughed to myself as I thought about how the enemy had me all in my feelings about the Pastor and his wife. I thought how if I had stayed in that place of bitterness women all over the church would not be blessed through the teaching that was going to go forth in our class. I blessed God for my deliverance.

Chapter 37

Deidra

I was nervous as I waited for this day. I could barely sleep the night before. I tossed and turned most of the night as I thought about the service. Today was the debut of the Hot Mess Choir. I smiled as I thought of how far we had come. I as always was up before my husband. I had my quiet time with Jesus and some coffee. I vowed that whatever happened I would not let it take away from what this day was truly about- unity.

I dressed and for the first time, Myron and I matched each other. I wore a green dress and he wore a gray suit with a green tie. As we drove to the church we talked about the year that we had at Holy Missionary. It had been one of ups and downs. Being a young couple at a very traditional church was not easy. We had to make sure we came dressed in the full armor of the Lord every day. We could laugh about it all now. We could even laugh about the Hot Mess Choir.

"I cannot believe they were going to fight at the first meeting." He said.

"Believe it, buddy, they were ready to fight! I can't believe nobody cussed as mad as everyone was. But, look at them now. They are one voice. They do all kinds of things together young and old. You know they went bowling the other night. I told them I could not make it but to have fun without me. I am so proud of them. They have proven to be leaders in the church."

"Are you excited about teaching?" Myron asked

"Yes, I am looking forward to working with Mother. I think I will learn a lot and the women will be blessed by both of our teachings. "

As we pulled up to the church I noticed that the parking lot was packed. It appeared that every member of Holy Missionary was in church today. If we were not the leaders of the church, we may not have had a place to park our car. I got out and headed to the choir room while Myron headed to his office.

"Where is Donnell?" I asked Stacey who I saw as I entered the room.

"He is taking Eva to the church nursery."

"Is everything okay between you two?"

"Yes." She said with a big smile.

I smiled and gave her a big hug. The choir began to put on their black and white robes. The children looked adorable in their little robes. I was pleased to see the Senior choir members helping the little kids get dressed. Everyone looked so wonderful. I could not help but let the tears flow.

"Don't cry Lady D, we are still your Hot Mess Choir, we just clean up well." One of the young adults said and the choir erupted in laughter.

We walked out of the choir room into the church and took our seat behind the pulpit in the choir stand. The church clapped for us as we walked out in our new robes. Myron wore a big smile. We may have been the Hot Mess Choir, but we did not look a mess. Our robes were black on the outside with a white stripe down the front.

"Before we get started there are a couple of announcements. Mother Odell and First Lady Deidra will have a class for the women starting next Saturday. The class will meet the first and third Saturday of each month. Amen. For all of you with young boys, I would like you to bring them out on Friday night to the boy's program led by minister in training Blake. Lastly, the choirs will have practice at their normal times however if you would like to join the Mass Choir you may do so by seeing First Lady Deidra. Now I will turn the service back over to our choir." Myron said.

I stood up and motioned to the choir to do the same. We began our selections with Myron's favorite song. His mouth flew open when he saw that I was singing the lead. He closed his eyes and tears slid down his chubby cheeks. Once that selection was done Stacey came up to sing her selection as the choir backed her up. Her voice caused goose bumps to appear on my arm. She sang the song from a special place in her soul every time she touched the microphone. I notice that Donnell could not stop smiling as she sang. After the choir's selections, Myron got up to speak.

"Many would question why I chose to speak on my anniversary. Church I come to tell you that although it is my anniversary today is not about me. It is about God and what God would have me to do. Amen."

He preached a mighty word. He started with the body and how although we are many parts we are all one. He preached until sweat poured down his face. The church was filled with praises as he brought forth the word of God. They shouted and waved their hands in the air.

After he was finished the choir sang their final selection. The twins' voices filled the church and there was not a dry eye in the church. Shonda their mother, was the first to let the tears flow. You could tell by the look of gratitude on her face she was happy. All her boys were working for or worshiping the Lord. I was so proud of her because she was an awesome woman of God. Her boys led the choir into worship. They ushered the church into an atmosphere that was one with Christ. I could not stop my own tears from flowing. God had transformed my heart, my choir, and the church.

The End

Acknowledgments

First and always I would like to thank God from whom all creativity flows. Without you Lord I am nothing and my words are in vain. I honestly cannot believe I am sitting here typing the acknowledgments for my fourth book. It is truly a blessing and I am humbled by the experience.

Several people asked me why I dedicate my book to You. They wondered who You was as if it could not be them. I dedicate each book to you because you are very important to me. You the reader are who I think about as God dictates the story I should write. I write for your edification and entertainment. I pray that somehow the characters have meant something to you and that you have been blessed in your reading.

I would like to thank my AIP family for their encouragement. I have the best pen sisters and pen brothers in the business. Their love and support are unmatched. I look forward to many more books as we grow together.

No book is complete without test readers known in some circles as Beta Readers. I would like to thank my team for enduring late-night emails and impromptu read this pleases and putting up with me. You guys are the best- ever I could not have done it without you. Although I choose to keep your identity secret please know that I love you.

I would be crazy if I did not thank the best husband in the world. Thank you for supporting my platform and helping me grow my business. Thank you for enduring long nights of me typing and long days of me worrying about what I typed lol. You are a blessing and you have made this process so easy. Thank you for allowing me to be me.

I would like to thank my girls for letting mommy work. I know that it is hard to understand at times why mommy is feverishly typing and talking to herself, but I appreciate your patience with another book. I thank you for all your help at my events and for being mom's angels.

I would like to thank my mother, auntie Beverly, and family for your support and encouragement. You are the best and I love you.

To my tribe and you know who you are: Y'all I did it again! Thank you for being there like nobody else. You ladies always got me, and I am grateful for you.

Well, SheReaders (that's what I call Y'all get it She Readers lol) until the next book I pray that you are blessed.

Happy Reading ⍰

Hot Mess Choir   She Nell

About She Nell

She Nell is a wife, mother, and daughter of the King. She lives in Tampa, Florida with her husband and three daughters. She is grateful that you decided to read her book.

Other Books by She Nell

A Good Thing

A good thing 2 If I be lifted up

A good thing 3 Vengeance is mine

#Blacklove Magic (Love in the streets heaven in the sheets)

33942825R00106

Made in the USA
Middletown, DE
20 January 2019